Grandad had only owned the fort for a few months. But he had big plans for it. He thought it was the perfect spot to start up his new enterprise – a Laughter Club, especially for children.

Smiler still couldn't get his head around that. The iron fort seemed like the worst place in the world for having a giggle. It made you feel grim just looking at it. It made your heart tighten too. It looked like the kind of place where nasty things happened.

As he watched, the whole fort glowed spooky-blue with lightning. Then sizzled and danced with blue flames. Every lightning bolt in heaven seemed to be aimed right at it!

Grandad's gonna be fried alive in his bed! thought Smiler, horrified.

Then he remembered the lightning conductors. The slim metal rods stuck up from the tops of the gun turrets. They should keep the fort safe. He'd thought, for a moment, it was going to turn into a giant electric fireball.

Phew, thought Smiler. I think the storm's

going out to sea. His heart stopped fluttering.

The thunder seemed fainter already.

The last, feeble lightning flash bounced off the top of a gun turret. The storm had fizzled out.

What's that? thought Smiler.

He'd been about to lower his binoculars. Now he gripped them so tightly his knuckles went bone-white.

'It's useless. I can't see a thing,' he muttered. The fort was the size of a cathedral. But it was lost in blackness. Even its warning light for ships seemed to have gone out.

Then the moon slipped out from behind a cloud.

Something was climbing the iron ladder up to the fort. The binoculars were going fuzzy. Frantically, Smiler tried to focus them. But it was too late. The moon was suddenly swallowed by clouds. When it got spat out again, Smiler took another look. There was nothing on the ladder.

What had it been?

Smiler answered his own question: 'Don't ask me.' Something squat and shambling?

But he'd had such a quick glimpse.

He shook his head, frowning. He checked again. Maybe, he decided, he'd seen nothing at all.

Chapter Two

Two weeks later, on the first day of his summer holidays, Smiler crossed the road from his house. He was going to walk to the iron fort. You could only do that at low tide. It meant crossing the mud flats. In some places, the mud was as sloppy as custard. It stank of dead crabs. But you were quite safe so long as you stayed on the big water pipe that went all the way out to the fort.

Smiler turned round and waved, 'Bye, Mum!' His mum waved back. She was watching him from a bedroom window.

He'd packed some clothes into his backpack. He planned to stay at the fort for a few days. Grandad was expecting him.

He had his joke book in his pocket. He

never went anywhere without it. He'd just added joke number 746 to his collection.

What's green, hairy and goes up and down?
Answer: A gooseberry in a lift

This was written in orange ink, only slightly above green ink on the laughter scale. It might raise a chuckle. But these days, Smiler couldn't be sure.

A terrible thing had happened. Smiler's joke book was letting him down. It had been his trusty friend for years and years, but lately he just couldn't depend on it.

Ever since he started school, Smiler had been the class clown. It gave him a buzz, being able to make other kids laugh. But now, in top juniors, he seemed to have lost the knack. Kids were getting sick of his jokes. They were getting sick of him! They'd groan when he took out his joke book: 'Not again!'

They'd even, especially the girls, say, 'Can't you *ever* stop being silly? Grow up!'

Smiler couldn't understand it. It really upset him. Why wasn't he popular any more? What was he doing wrong?

Even his nickname seemed like a bad joke. These days he scowled more than he smiled.

Smiler sighed. He didn't want to join Grandad's Laughter Club. He wasn't in the mood. But he'd promised Grandad. It was the official opening tomorrow. The first members would be arriving.

'*Whoops!*'

He wasn't concentrating. His foot had slipped off the water pipe. Greedily, the mud sucked it in. It sank through the greasy crust into the black, tarry stuff beneath. Wobbling about on the pipe, his arms going like windmills, Smiler tried snatching his foot back. The mud wouldn't let it go.

He started to panic: 'Help!'

He toppled over, sprawling across the pipe with one leg still trapped in the mud. The mud had swallowed his leg up to the knee. Frantically, Smiler tried to tug it free. But the mud gripped him like a python. He gave up, exhausted.

Smiler twisted round. Was Mum still at the bedroom window? Even if she was, she couldn't see him without binoculars. He was too far from the shore, a tiny figure lost in a vast landscape of mud flats and racing clouds. But he wasn't near enough to the iron fort. If he shouted, Grandad wouldn't hear him.

Smiler hugged the pipe. He rested. Ages seemed to pass. He gave his leg a few more hopeless tugs. It didn't budge. It might as well have been set in concrete.

Smiler groaned. So what was he going to do now? Why did the sky over the fort look like raspberry ripple, all streaked with red? Shocked, Smiler thought, I haven't been stuck that long, have I? Sunset was coming. Soon it would be dark.

'Help!' he screamed. 'Help!' But only squawking seagulls answered him. He gave up. He slumped over the pipe and closed his eyes.

When he opened them again, something caught his attention. What was that sparkling silver ribbon? It was on the horizon, far beyond the iron fort. Then he realized. It was the sea sneaking in.

'Help! I'm stuck!'

His voice was hysterical now. Once it got started, the sea came speeding into the estuary like a bullet train. Loads of people had been trapped and drowned. There were terrible stories. Like the one about the family of circus clowns taking a short cut across the mud flats. They'd been hired to entertain at the birthday party of a rich little girl who lived on the other side of the estuary. They got stuck in the mud, with the tide coming in.

'Don't think about it!' Smiler told himself.

But he couldn't help it. Sometimes, people said, when the wind was in the right direction, you could hear despairing laughter. It was the clowns. Telling each other jokes to keep their spirits up, while they waited to drown –

'What's brown and sticky?' Smiler said out loud in a trembling voice.

'A stick,' he answered himself shakily. But telling himself that joke only made him more desperate. With all his strength, Smiler gave his leg a great heave. It wouldn't shift.

'Stupid useless leg!'

He was crying now, his face pressed against the pipe. Around him, the sea was bubbling up through the worm holes. The channels in the mud flats were already racing with gurgling water.

I'm going to drown! thought Smiler, terrified. Like those clowns.

Then he looked up. Through his tears he saw something spectacular. The setting sun had hit the fort and made it magical. The gun turrets sparkled like crimson towers. The metal plates on the outside glowed like rubies. Smiler had to shield his eyes, it was so dazzling. Like the night of the storm, you could almost feel the fort's power, reaching out . . .

'Try again,' a voice in his head told him.

Smiler yanked at his leg. The mud gave a slurpy belch and his foot popped straight out. No problem at all.

My white trainer! was Smiler's first thought. It's ruined! It's full of that stinking mud!

It was a crazy thing to worry about when he'd just almost drowned. After he'd worn them for a week, his shoes smelled like dead crabs anyway.

'Just get moving,' he ordered himself. This was no time to hang about. The sea was so close he could hear its low, angry growl. He scooted along that pipe as if a pack of hungry wolves was chasing him.

By the time he reached the fort, the sun had gone down. There was nothing magical about it now. It loomed above him on its stilty iron legs, as massive and ugly as a multi-storey car park. Its armour-plated body was warty with all sorts of weird junk. Gun turrets, lookout towers – bits added on during two World Wars. It was vast inside too – a maze of metal rooms and corridors. Smiler had been here twice before. But he'd only explored a tiny bit of it.

A face peered over from the landing stage. Even in this fuzzy greyness, Smiler could see it looked worried.

'Where *were* you?' said Grandad. 'I was just going to call up the coast guard.'

'I'm all right,' said Smiler. 'I got held up, that's all.'

Grandad didn't get mad. He just commented, 'You cut it a bit fine,' as the first frothy wave from the rising tide swirled under the fort.

The mud gave way to a stretch of firm

sand. It was safe for Smiler to step off the pipe. He walked over to the iron ladder that went up to the landing stage and found himself staring at a big slab of toffee-coloured rock.

'Hey,' said Smiler, 'there's rock under this fort.'

'Why do you think they built it here?' Grandad called down. 'Good, solid foundations!'

'But I didn't see rock when I came before,' said Smiler. 'There was just sand here.'

'It was that massive storm two weeks ago,' said Grandad. 'It shifted tons of sand about. That's when the rock got uncovered.'

'I think there are some kind of footprints here!' Fat seaweed pods popped under Smiler's shoes as he walked over to investigate.

'They're fossils!' said Smiler, excited. He squatted down. There was a track of them across the rock. And they ended abruptly. As if whatever had made them had been lifted up into the air.

He traced the fossil footprints with his finger. They were a weird shape. He couldn't work out what made them.

'What kind of footprints?' came Grandad's puzzled voice from above.

'I dunno,' said Smiler, frowning. 'Some kind of giant frog?'

Grandad laughed. He thought Smiler was joking. Even when he was being deadly serious, people often thought Smiler was joking.

'And there are limpet shells all round them,' said Smiler, staring at a scattering of yellow shells, like little Chinese hats.

Nothing very scary about them. But for some reason, Smiler felt a chilly tingle chase down his spine.

'The fossil footprints of a giant frog that eats limpets?' laughed Grandad. 'Archaeologists would pay a fortune to see that!'

'The limpet shells aren't fossils!' Smiler protested. 'They're fresh ones!'

The shambling shape, the one he'd seen climbing the ladder on the night of the storm, suddenly flashed through Smiler's mind. 'But that didn't look anything like a frog,' he murmured to himself. And, anyway, hadn't he already decided he didn't see anything?

Grandad was getting impatient. 'You staying down there all night? I don't like to mention it, but the sea's coming in. And I've got pepperoni pizza in the freezer.'

Smiler glanced up. You could scarcely see Grandad through the gloom but Smiler just knew he'd be wearing his jeans and trainers and shabby old American Air Force flying jacket.

'My grandad's quite cool – for a grandad,' Smiler sometimes told his friends. In his spare time, Grandad played guitar in a rock band with some other grandads. He had lots of lady friends. Smiler's dad disapproved. He said Grandad was far too old to be carrying on like that.

Waves were sloshing over the rock. His white trainers were soaking up water like sponges.

Mum's going to say, 'Look at the state of those!' thought Smiler.

It was time to climb. Smiler paddled over to the iron ladder and started hauling himself up it. The rungs were slimy with seaweed and spiky with limpets.

As soon as he hoisted himself on to the

landing stage, he forgot about the strange, webbed footprints because Grandad started telling him a joke.

'This guy goes on a television quiz show. He's only got two questions to answer and he wins a million pounds. Right?' said Grandad.

'Right,' said Smiler, warily. Grandad's jokes were usually weedy green ones. Sometimes, they were even worse than that. Smiler didn't even have a colour for them. Plus, they went on for ages. You'd forgotten the beginning by the time he got to the end.

'Anyway, the quizmaster asks him the first question: "Which of the following birds does NOT build its own nest. A lark, a sparrow, a cuckoo or a starling?"

'And the guy says, "I know this one! It's *definitely* a cuckoo."

'"Brilliant!" says the quizmaster. "We've got a real superbrain here! And now, for a *million* pounds, can you tell us WHY a lark, a sparrow and a starling build nests, but a cuckoo doesn't need to?"

'"That's easy," says the guy. "Because a cuckoo lives in a clock."'

Smiler felt his mouth tugging upwards, ever so slightly. But he kept his face solemn.

'*Awwww*, Grandad,' he groaned. 'That's terrible.' Though, privately, he was thinking, I'll pinch that and write it down later.

It was nearer bog standard than gold standard. It would take up three pages of his joke book. But it might make some of his mates chuckle. Then they'd stop complaining, 'Smiler, you're just not *funny* any more!'

Chapter Three

Grandad was waving his slice of pizza about. He always got carried away whenever he talked about Laughter Club. He'd been planning it for ages – ever since he retired from teaching.

'It's just what an over-worked, stressed-out school kid needs!' he was saying. 'Leave those pushy parents behind! Forget about tests and homework for a whole week! *Find Time to Smile!*'

That was one of the slogans Grandad had made up for Laughter Club. He'd put it in all his adverts.

'Laughter is absolutely essential,' declared Grandad. 'Did you know there are loads of Laughter Clubs in India? But mine is the first one in this country especially for kids.'

Smiler didn't want to crush Grandad's enthusiasm, but he had some major doubts about Laughter Club. 'I don't know many kids who can't *smile*,' Grandad,' he protested.

'It's not that they *can't*,' said Grandad. 'It's just that some seem to have forgotten how to. Wait until you meet Coriander Jackson, our first club member. Then you'll see what I mean.'

Smiler moved on to his other main worry. 'This fort –' he began, looking around at the grim, grey metal walls of the kitchen where they were eating their pizza.

'I know what you're going to say,' Grandad interrupted him eagerly. 'You're going to say that it's a bit too cut off, a bit too remote.'

Smiler hadn't planned to say that. He'd planned to say, 'It's about as giggle-making as being in a graveyard. And just as spooky.'

'But that's what these kids *need*,' Grandad went raving on. 'To be right away from the pressures of modern life. No busy after-school schedule. No piano grades to pass. No extra maths lessons –'

Smiler butted in with another question.

'Grandad, exactly *how* are you going to make these kids laugh? It's not that easy.' Smiler knew that from personal experience. 'Kids won't laugh at just anything. Kids these days have a very sophisticated sense of humour.'

'Sausages!' shouted Grandad, suddenly.

'Sausages?' repeated Smiler, his face already twitching into a grin.

'See, I made *you* smile,' said Grandad, 'just by shouting "Sausages!" I thought you said kids these days had a sophisticated sense of humour?'

'They do,' said Smiler, glumly. 'It's just me that doesn't.'

Smiler didn't feel sleepy. Before he went to bed, he wandered back out on to the landing stage. Because it was high tide, the fort's big warning light for ships had come on. It made it as bright as day out here.

The water was thirty metres deep under the fort now. Smiler looked over the railings. The swirling currents made him feel dizzy. Seaweed, fixed to the fort's legs, spread out like the frizzy green hair of a drowned clown. Smiler shuddered.

What are those? he thought. Long, sinister

shadows swam right beneath him. Conga eels! Grandad said they lived under the fort. They were writhing in slippery knots around the iron ladder.

Smiler thought of the night of the storm. And the figure he'd seen climbing that ladder. Why couldn't he get it out of his mind? Maybe he'd ask Grandad at breakfast if he'd had any strange visitors.

Back in his bedroom, Smiler put his joke book under his pillow. It hadn't been much help lately. His friends even made fun of it. But he couldn't quite give it up. He needed it like a baby needs its comfort blanket.

He tried to settle down in his creaky iron bed. The fort was hardly a five-star hotel. He hoped Coriander Jackson wasn't too fussy.

What's that noise? thought Smiler, suddenly waking up, just after midnight.

The fort always echoed with sounds. The sea crashed into it, the wind battered it. Bits of loose metal clattered and clanged. It was like being shut up inside a giant tin can while someone banged the outside with a big stick. Smiler knew all the fort's everyday noises.

But this one was different.

Smiler went to his door and opened it. A metal corridor stretched into the distance. It was lit with low, flickering yellow lights.

The sound came drifting down the corridor again. Piping notes, like someone playing a flute.

Where's that coming from? thought Smiler, half-scared, half-spellbound. It was so sweet, so wistful, that without thinking, he stepped out from the safety of his bedroom into the corridor. He just had to track down that music.

He was like an enchanted child, following the Pied Piper. His bare feet made only a faint slapping sound on the metal. He climbed iron staircases, padded down passages, where lights glowed, sickly yellow. It took all his concentration, trying to pick out the flute from all the other sounds the fort made. He didn't notice he'd strayed into unfamiliar territory. He didn't even notice the stern sign that warned him:

HEALTH HAZARD!
NO PEOPLE BEYOND THIS POINT!

The flute stopped.

'*Awwwww,*' said Smiler, sadly.

He stopped too, in front of an iron door. He put his ear to the metal. He listened.

'I *think* it came from behind there,' he murmured.

The door had two heavy iron bolts top and bottom. Whoever was behind it couldn't get out.

Smiler waited for the flute to start up again. It didn't. He looked around him.

I'm lost, he realized. Should he try to shift those bolts? Should he try to find his way back? All these corridors looked the same . . .

He was just wondering what to do when he heard a loud slap-slapping noise in the distance. It echoed through the spooky corridors. It was much louder than the sound of his own steps. Something with very big feet was approaching.

Smiler forgot about the flute music. He shrank back against the bolted door. Who was coming? He thought of those webbed fossil footprints in the rock. But they must be thousands of years old! Then he thought of the ape-like figure he'd seen clinging to the ladder. All sorts of wild ideas whirled through his head. None of them made any sense.

Slap, slap, slap, slap.

Smiler wished he'd remembered his joke book. It wasn't that he'd suddenly thought of a rib-tickling joke to write down. It was that, somehow, having it with him always made him feel braver.

The footsteps came very close. *Slap.* Then suddenly stopped.

Smiler strained his eyes, trying to see through the gloom. What was that, poking round the corner? It was the toes of two green lace-up shoes, spotted with pink dots. They were very long toes. They stayed dead still – as if whatever was lurking there had forgotten its feet would stick out.

'It can't be!' gasped Smiler, horrified. Nightmare thoughts flapped like bats in his brain. He felt sick.

The feet were on the move. They shuffled further out. Then a bit further. Were those shoes never-ending?

'*Aaaargh!*' Smiler saw baggy trousers, frizzy orange hair, a red nose. His most hideous fears had come true. The iron fort was haunted! By evil drowned clowns!

Smiler ran, fleeing in panic through a maze of grey metal tunnels. *Slap, slap, slap, slap.* Those green spotty shoes pounded after him. The ghost clown was gaining!

Smiler stumbled, fell. He cowered on the cold metal floor, covering his head with both hands.

An anxious voice above him said, 'Oh dear! Have you hurt yourself? I'm Mr Funny Bones, Laughter Club's clown. *Guaranteed to keep you chuckling!*'

Smiler felt himself being helped to his feet.

'Pleased to meet you,' Mr Funny Bones said, holding out a hand as cold and clammy as a wet fish.

Chapter Four

'Grandad!' said Smiler angrily at breakfast. 'Why didn't you tell me you'd hired a clown?'

Two things infuriated him. One, he'd had a shocking scare last night when Mr Funny Bones popped up out of nowhere. And two, if Grandad wanted to hire someone to make kids laugh, why didn't he give the job to his own grandson?

It's the one thing I'm really good at, thought Smiler. I've got seven hundred and forty-six jokes in my collection. But then he remembered that, despite this, he'd been a complete loser lately where making other kids laugh was concerned.

'I *meant* to say something,' said Grandad vaguely. 'I've just got so much on my mind.

Setting up Laughter Club has hardly been a big hoot, you know. Hundreds of forms to fill in, dozens of checks, inspections. I thought I'd left all that behind when I retired.'

'Well, I don't like him,' insisted Smiler. 'He's got shifty eyes. And he's really sweaty.'

He'd only been with the clown for five minutes, while Mr Funny Bones gave him directions back to his bedroom. But already Smiler had decided there was something slippery about him. Like the eels that twisted and twined around the iron ladder. And besides, what was he doing, sneaking around the fort at midnight?

'And does he wear that clown costume *all* the time?' asked Smiler. 'And that freaky clown make-up? It's weird.'

Smiler had spent nearly his whole life being a comedian. But, for some reason, he didn't find clowns funny. He thought they were sinister and scary.

Grandad shrugged: 'Maybe he's just getting into the mood. He takes clowning *seriously*! He's a well-qualified young man. He's got a degree in Laughter Studies from the University of Middle England.'

Grandad went waffling on about Mr Funny Bones' clowning qualifications. Impatiently, Smiler chipped in. 'Come clean, Grandad,' he demanded. 'Is there anyone else sharing this fort with us? I mean, *besides* Mr Funny Bones?'

He was thinking about the flute player behind the bolted door. And that monkey shape crouching on the ladder. That hadn't been Mr Funny Bones. The clown was long and skinny, like a string bean.

Grandad looked uneasy. It was high tide. Waves, whacking against the fort's legs, filled the silence.

'Actually, Smiler,' began Grandad, as if he'd decided to get something off his chest. Then he suddenly looked at his watch and sprang up out of his seat. '*Oops*, must get the motor boat revved up! I'm off to the mainland to fetch Coriander and her parents.'

Smiler met him on the landing stage ten minutes later. 'Grandad!' he said, disapprovingly. 'You look smart!'

Grandad had taken off his sloppy 'Born to Rock' T-shirt. He'd put on a smart blue shirt and matching stripy tie.

'You look like you're going to read the news!' said Smiler. 'I thought this Laughter Club was supposed to be all relaxed and easy-going and groovy?'

'It is,' Grandad answered through tight lips. 'But I've got the feeling that Coriander's parents aren't.'

'They're not staying, are they?'

'I hope not,' Grandad frowned. 'They're just seeing Coriander settled in. I want to get shot of *them* as soon as I can.'

Smiler waved as the Laughter Club motor boat *phut-phutted* away. Since he was last here, Grandad had painted another slogan on it:

YOUR DAY GOES THE WAY THE CORNERS OF YOUR MOUTH TURN!

Smiler groaned. He shouted out, 'Grandad, that's really cheesy!'

But Grandad was too far away to hear him.

The sea was sparkling today. The sky was a big, blue bowl. Even the iron fort didn't look so grim.

But Smiler didn't have time to admire the scenery. He plunged once again into the dim, cave-like corridors of the iron fort. He was on a mission. He wanted to find the flute player. He was sure, by now, that Grandad was hiding something from him.

This time, there was no flute to guide him. He tried to remember his way back, but the fort was a maze of grey metal tunnels. He couldn't tell one from another.

This is useless! Smiler was thinking. I'm never going to find that bolted door again.

Then he heard a familiar sound: s*lap, slap, slap, slap.*

Smiler pressed himself flat against the iron walls. Mr Funny Bones tippy-toed across at the end of the corridor, looking over his shoulder.

What's he up to? thought Smiler, as he crept after him. Sneaking about like a spy. And doesn't he *ever* take off that clown disguise? It's like he doesn't want to be recognized.

Mr Funny Bones stopped. Smiler shrank back.

It's hard work trying to tiptoe when you're wearing long clown's shoes. It's like walking on stilts. Mr Funny Bones rested for a second. He fumbled in his baggy pants for a tissue to dry his soggy palms. Those shifty eyes were skittering about like marbles.

At last, Mr Funny Bones tip-toed off again. He passed by a sign that shrieked,

HEALTH HAZARD!
NO PEOPLE BEYOND THIS POINT!

Smiler hesitated. What's all that about then? he wondered, as he read the sign. But Mr Funny Bones was getting away. Smiler hurried after him.

Mr Funny Bones stopped again. This time, by a porthole set into a metal wall. He couldn't get close enough because of his big clown's shoes. So he had to look in sideways. He seemed to be squinting through the glass for a very long time.

He muttered something: '*What are you up to?*' Then he loped away into the gloom, without once looking back.

Smiler took Mr Funny Bone's place at the porthole. He too peered through it. But he could get his nose right up against the glass.

It seemed to be some kind of laboratory. He saw computers. And scientific equipment on shiny steel benches. There were some big glass fish tanks. What was in them?

'Jellyfish!' breathed Smiler.

They were violet, pink, blue, all the colours of the rainbow. Some trailed frilly tentacles behind them. Some opened and closed, like tiny see-through umbrellas. But inside every one of them, tiny green lights were twinkling.

'That's beautiful,' sighed Smiler.

Whose jellyfish collection was it? He could have watched them for ages, drifting up and down. It was strangely soothing. But he tore his eyes away. He had come to find the flute player. And he hadn't much time. Grandad would be back in a minute, with Coriander and her parents. And Smiler had promised he would be there.

Along the corridor, he found what he was looking for. The bolted door. He put his ear to the metal. It was quiet as a grave in there. The bottom of the door had rusted away. There was a gap. Smiler flung himself full length on the floor and peered through it. But all he could see was darkness.

'Is there anybody in there?' he cried.

Like a sad little message, something came rolling under the door. It was a single limpet shell. Smiler trapped it under his hand.

Clang! A door further down the corridor burst open. Clutching the limpet shell, Smiler scrambled to his feet. What he saw made his heart chill with horror.

Through the dim yellow light, something monstrous came looming. What was it? It had white, wrinkly skin. A white, wrinkly, bald head. It looked like a Giant Maggot, two metres tall!

The Maggot towered above him. Its skin seemed to ripple and squirm. It had no face, just a black mask that ended in a short, piggy snout.

Smiler's legs went rubbery. He thought he would crash to the floor.

A gasping sound came out of the snout. What was it saying? Smiler's panicky brain just couldn't interpret it.

The menacing voice hissed again.

It said, '*Sssssssssssss*. Something nasty – *sssssssss* – happened to me when I was a little –'

But Smiler was too far away to hear. He was running, his feet drumming on metal, his arms flapping like a swan trying to take off. Past the **HEALTH HAZARD** warning, back through the maze of tunnels. Was it after him? He stopped, his chest burning, his brain a red blur. He looked back.

The shadowy corridor stretched into the distance. It was empty. He'd escaped.

'*Phew!*' He sank to his knees. Slowly, the blood stopped *whooshing* in his ears.

Why did Grandad buy this dump? he thought for the thousandth time. How can you run a Laughter Club in a house of horrors? Laughter Club was supposed to be stress free!

I've had more stress since yesterday tea time than in my whole life, thought Smiler.

But it wasn't over yet. He'd just checked the corridor again.

'It's cool, Smiler,' he told himself. 'Don't panic.' It wasn't the Giant Maggot down there. But there *was* something else moving. It didn't look big or dangerous. But it was coming closer. And it was glowing bright green like the jellyfish in the tank.

Smiler rubbed his eyes. 'All this stress is driving me crazy,' he decided. It couldn't be what he thought it was. His eyes must be playing tricks. 'It's a –. It's a –' Smiler stuttered. The word just wouldn't come out of his mouth.

Then a voice behind him helpfully finished his sentence for him.

'It's a rabbit.'

Smiler jerked his head up. His astonished gaze looked right into the jiggling eyes of Mr Funny Bones.

For the second time in just a few hours Mr Funny Bones helped him up and dusted him down. This time, Smiler didn't even notice his dripping palms.

Scared by their voices, the glowing green rabbit had turned round again and hopped off.

'I think I'm going mad!' said Smiler, smacking himself violently on the forehead as if to drive out those loony demons.

Mr Funny Bones looked deeply concerned. 'Don't do that. You might get brain damage.' His brow wrinkled under his chalk-white clown make-up. 'Hasn't your grandad told you that we're sharing this fort with someone else?'

'Who with? The flute player behind the bolted door?'

As he said this, Smiler unclenched his fist. He was still holding the limpet shell. It seemed to him that it had been sent under the door as an SOS. He slipped it into his pocket.

'So you heard that haunting music too?' said Mr Funny Bones, his eyes narrowing. 'But no, it wasn't the flute player I was talking about.'

'You mean the thing that looks like a monster maggot?'

'That's her,' said Mr Funny Bones.

'Her?' repeated Smiler, in a dazed voice. He tried a few tottering steps forward. 'I hope you don't mind me asking or anything. But was that a glowing green rabbit I saw just now?'

'What else could it be?' asked Mr Funny Bones, as if Smiler shouldn't be surprised to see a fluorescent bunny hopping around the iron fort. His voice sank to a whisper. 'That's *her* doing,' he told Smiler. 'It's because of her experiments with jellyfish.'

'Experiments?' demanded Smiler, desperately. 'With jellyfish? I don't understand. Who is *she*? What's that rabbit got to do with it? Just tell me what's going on!'

'Don't worry,' said Mr Funny Bones, looking over his shoulder and keeping his voice low. 'There's a perfectly simple explanation. I'm going to say one word that will make it all crystal clear. And that magic word is: NITS.'

'Pardon?'

'Nits,' hissed Mr Funny Bones. 'They're the eggs of head lice. Haven't you ever caught head lice at school?'

Of course Smiler had. Several times. Although he didn't happen to have them at the moment. But just the mention of head lice was enough to set him scratching.

One hand still busy scratching his head, Smiler opened his mouth. He had about a hundred fresh questions to ask.

But he only had time for one, 'What are you *talking* about?' Suddenly, through an open porthole, came the *phut, phut, phut* of the motor boat chugging back.

'Oh, dear,' said Mr Funny Bones, flapping

his sweaty palms about and becoming instantly jittery. 'There's your grandad coming back with Coriander Jackson and her parents.'

'I've got to be there!' shouted Smiler, dashing away. 'I promised Grandad!'

Just when Smiler had never felt less like laughing in his life, Laughter Club was about to start.

Chapter Five

When Smiler reached the landing stage, Coriander Jackson and her parents had just climbed up the iron ladder. They looked a bit green from their bumpy sea trip in the motor boat. But Mrs Jackson soon recovered.

She took a sharp look around the fort. She pursed her lips. '*Hummm,*' she said. She didn't sound impressed.

Then she turned on Grandad. 'Where is your timetable of activities?' she interrogated him sternly.

'But that's where Laughter Club is different. We don't have a timetable,' replied Grandad, proudly. 'It's the whole idea. NO pressure! We spend our time *wasting* time. Just generally laughing our socks off and being silly.'

'*No pressure?*' asked Mr Jackson, puzzled, as if Grandad came from a different planet. '*Wasting time?*'

Mrs Jackson chipped in, sounding smug. 'We *never* waste time, do we, Coriander? We spend every second of our day usefully. From breakfast until bedtime. Even after school Coriander does extra maths and takes mandolin lessons and learns Mandarin.'

Coriander said nothing. No expression crossed her unsmiling face. It might have been made out of marble.

'Did you just say "*being silly*"?' repeated Mr Jackson, as if he was still struggling to understand the meaning of the words.

Coriander spoke for the first time: 'Silliness is for *children*,' she said, scornfully

'Phew, *that's* all right then,' Smiler blurted out. 'All those school reports I got that said, "This boy must stop being silly!" I mean, I thought I was doing something *wrong*!'

Grandad shot him a look that said, 'Shut up!'

Smiler's hands went up slyly to scratch his head. Ever since Mr Funny Bones mentioned head lice he just couldn't help it. Coriander's mum gave him a suspicious look. Smiler jammed his hands under his armpits – that should stop them.

'I've made a *big* mistake,' Grandad was thinking frantically. He should never have mentioned silliness. Coriander's parents obviously didn't approve. If he wasn't careful, they'd take Coriander away. And he'd lose his first, in fact his *only*, Laughter Club member.

'If everyone went around being silly and giggling all day,' said Mrs Jackson sternly, 'nothing would get done, would it, Coriander?'

Coriander's face stayed like stone. Even her eyes didn't flicker. No one could tell what she was thinking.

But Grandad was doing some rapid rethinking. 'Actually, laughter is a very *serious* business,' he said. 'Being able to laugh helps children in all areas of their life. Especially with *passing exams.*'

This time, he'd pressed the right button. 'Is that right?' said Mr Jackson, his nose quivering keenly.

'Passing exams is very important to us, isn't it, Coriander?' said Mrs Jackson.

'Lots of research proves it!' Grandad continued confidently. He was pretty sure now he could win them over. 'We at Laughter Club teach the things that school doesn't. We will help make your child into a many-sided child –'

'Then make me into a dodecahedron!' shouted Smiler. He just couldn't help it.

'Pardon?' said Mr and Mrs Jackson, turning blank faces towards him.

'It's a joke,' Smiler told them, grinning.

'A *joke*?' frowned Mr and Mrs Jackson, as if they'd never heard the word before.

'Grandad said about making a *many-sided* child,' said Smiler. 'So *I* said make me into a *dodecahedron* cos that's got *twelve* sides and . . .' Smiler's voice trailed away into silence. He stopped grinning. It wasn't a very funny joke in the first place. But trying to explain it totally wrecked it. 'Just forget it,' he mumbled, staring down at his shoes.

Me and my big mouth, he was thinking, his ears burning red with shame. It was just another example of the way his joke-telling talent was going down the drain.

He took the limpet shell out of his pocket

and started to fiddle about with it, just to keep himself busy so his mouth wouldn't misbehave. He noticed something about it he hadn't seen before. The limpet shell had two tiny holes in it, one on each side. They were really neat. Had somebody drilled them? It looked as if the shell was meant to be threaded on string.

'And one last thing,' said Grandad, who was still trying to sell Laughter Club to Mr and Mrs Jackson, 'when Coriander leaves we'll give her a certificate. It says, "This week I learned to laugh."'

Mrs Jackson's eyes lit up. She wasn't convinced yet that learning to laugh would make Coriander top of the class, but she loved certificates. You could put them on walls. Then boast about them to other parents.

'We collect certificates, don't we, Coriander?' she said, approvingly.

Great, thought Grandad, who'd just pulled that certificate idea out of thin air. I think I've got them hooked.

Just to make extra sure, he pointed to Smiler. 'Here's one of our success stories,' he said. 'Just by learning to laugh, this boy got top marks in maths!'

Smiler was ready for this. He had his instructions. He grinned at everyone like a village idiot.

Coriander looked scornful. She seemed to suspect it was some kind of set-up.

But Mr and Mrs Jackson were impressed. If Laughter Club could make this bubble-brain a better student, it could turn Coriander into a genius!

Under the anxious eyes of Grandad, Mr and Mrs Jackson had a whispered conversation about Laughter Club.

'I don't like this *no stress* thing,' said Mr Jackson. 'If children aren't stressed, they're not working hard enough.'

'But,' Mrs Jackson reminded him, 'Coriander's teacher did recommend a week at Laughter Club.'

'Yes, she said she needed to, what was it, to *chill out*?' added Mr Jackson, shaking his head as if he was mystified.

'And if it helps her pass exams, it's worth every penny.'

'Besides, we haven't got anything else

fixed for this first week. Not since that algebra course was cancelled. It's the only bit of her holidays that isn't filled up.'

'That settles it then,' they both agreed.

'Bye-bye, Coriander, see you on Saturday,' said Coriander's dad.

'We'll be checking up on you!' warned her mum. 'So keep your mobile switched on!'

'*Errr,*' said Grandad, apologetically. 'Mobiles don't work very well in the iron fort. It's all this metal. Sometimes, you might not be able to get through.'

Did Coriander look relieved? *Naa*, thought Smiler. You're imagining it. Her face was as frosty as ever.

Grandad hustled her parents back down the iron ladder before they could change their minds about Laughter Club.

Coriander didn't wave. Was she sad or pleased they were going? Who could tell?

'I won't be long!' Grandad shouted up from the motor boat. 'Smiler, you and Mr Funny Bones entertain Coriander until I get back.'

The motor boat *phut-phutted* away into the distance.

Smiler looked around desperately. Where was Mr Funny Bones? He was getting paid to do this sort of thing!

There was no sign of him. Smiler thought, Oh no, I'm on my own! He took a sneaky look at Coriander. She stared stonily back at him.

Her face dared him, 'Go on, make me laugh.'

Smiler gulped, nervously. He didn't know where to start. He tried to remember Grandad's cuckoo-clock joke. But it had gone clean out of his head. So had every one of the 746 jokes in his collection. Except one.

'What's brown and sticky?' he asked her, desperately.

This time, Coriander's look of scorn was withering. 'Are you *serious*?' she asked him.

Smiler shrank inside. It was happening again! Just like at school. Soon she'd be saying, 'Grow up!'

Just then a pair of clown shoes came clattering out on to the landing stage. They were green with pink spots. Mr Funny Bones had finally shown up. He was carrying a large cardboard suitcase.

Smiler never thought he'd be so pleased to see the creepy clown. 'Over to you, Mr Funny Bones!' he cried, with a huge, private '*Phew!*' of relief.

Mr Funny Bones leapt into action. He fumbled with a hidden switch and made his bow tie go round.

'Do I see a tiny chuckle?' he asked Coriander. 'Or even a big *ho ho ho*? Look! This is how you do it!' Mr Funny Bones held his shaking stomach with both hands. 'Now tell Mr Funny Bones,' he coaxed Coriander, 'when did you last have a really good laugh?'

'Is this some kind of *test*?' asked Coriander suspiciously. 'Will there be an *exam* at the end of it?'

'Heavens, no!' cried Mr Funny Bones, shocked. 'We don't do that kind of thing at Laughter Club. We do things like *this*!'

He fumbled with his bow tie again and this time it lit up with a feeble, twinkling light.

'Clowns are for *children*,' said Coriander, contemptuously.

Mr Funny Bones couldn't understand it. The revolving bow-tie routine always went down a storm at old folk's homes. Which were the only places so far he'd done any clowning.

Smiler knew how Mr Funny Bones felt. He was secretly squirming too. 'That Coriander thinks you're really uncool!' a mocking voice told him, inside his head. 'She thinks you're an irritating little pest.'

'I don't care what she thinks!' he tried to argue with himself. 'She's snooty. She hasn't got a sense of humour!' But, to his own annoyance, he did care.

Mr Funny Bones wiped his sweaty forehead. It seemed to be spraying more than a lawn sprinkler.

Oh dear, he was thinking. That didn't go down very well. Making kids laugh was going to be much harder than he thought.

'Am I the *only* one with any sense of humour around here?' Smiler asked himself. He let his head fall hopelessly into his hands. 'How did I get myself into this situation?' Stuck on an iron fort with the worst clown in the world and a girl who couldn't smile, even if her life depended on it.

Not to mention the Giant Maggot, the

mysterious flute player, the green glowing rabbit and several other problems. But he didn't want to scramble his brain even more by thinking about those just now. Coriander was quite enough to deal with at the moment.

Mr Funny Bones was taking a twitchy look over his shoulder. He seemed to have forgotten why he was here, as if he had other, more urgent, things on his mind.

Hurry up and come back, Grandad! Smiler was thinking.

Suddenly Mr Funny Bones seemed to snap to attention. 'I need a volunteer for my next trick!' he cried. He looked hopefully at Coriander. Her stony face stared back. 'Don't even *think* about it!' it seemed to be saying.

He looked pleadingly at Smiler. Strangely, Smiler took a few paces forward. To his own surprise, he felt quite sorry for Mr Funny Bones. Smiler knew what it felt like to be a loser where making kids laugh was concerned.

'As a serious student of clowning,' began Mr Funny Bones, boringly, 'I am going to demonstrate some traditional jolly japes used by clowns throughout the ages to make audiences laugh until they cried. Number one – the custard-pie fight.'

He opened his suitcase, rummaged around inside and brought out a big custard pie. It was bright yellow and wobbly.

Now we're getting somewhere! thought Smiler. Even Coriander might squeeze out a tiny *tee-hee* at this.

He screwed his eyes tightly shut and waited for the custard attack.

Nothing happened. He opened his eyes. Mr Funny Bones was still standing there, holding the pie.

'What are you waiting for?' demanded Smiler. 'Slam it in my face! Go on!'

'Oh, I couldn't do that!' said Mr Funny Bones, shocked. 'That would be too unkind. And while I'm thinking about it,' added Mr Funny Bones, 'watch out for that banana skin I've just dropped. You might trip over it.'

'You're not supposed to *warn* me about it!' said Smiler, throwing his arms out, hopelessly.

Mr Funny Bones looked horrified. 'But you might be badly hurt!' he protested.

And, in a flash, Smiler realized why Mr Funny Bones was a clowning disaster. He was a bag of nerves. Look, he was wringing his hands out like sponges. But the main reason was that he wasn't cruel enough. A real clown would have let Smiler slip on that banana skin. He wouldn't have helped him up. He would have hooted with laughter even if he was lying there with a broken leg!

'Forget all this knockabout stuff,' Smiler advised him, as one funny-man to another. 'You're no good at it. Do you know any jokes?'

Neither of them noticed that their audience had wandered away. Coriander was hanging over the landing-stage rails, staring down at the waves. Her face gave nothing away. She seemed to be in a world of her own.

'Jokes?' frowned Mr Funny Bones. 'Now, let me see. *Ahhh*, I know. What's brown and sticky?'

'Don't you know any funnier ones than that?' wailed Smiler. 'It bombed when I just told it! You need some help from my faithful old joke book!'

Then he remembered. That faithful old joke book had been letting him down badly lately.

'But that's quite an interesting joke to analyse,' insisted Mr Funny Bones. 'The humour is based upon two different meanings of the word *sticky*. The person who hears the joke naturally assumes that *sticky* means "a gummy, gluey substance". Whereas, for the purposes of this joke it actually means "stick-like", so –'

'NO, NO, NO!' shrieked Smiler, almost tearing his hair out. 'Don't you know the most basic rules of being funny? Never, *ever*, try to explain jokes! It just kills them stone dead!'

Mr Funny Bones shuffled his big clown shoes and looked ashamed.

'You're not a *real* clown, are you?' said Smiler.

'How did you guess?' asked Mr Funny Bones.

Mr Funny Bones looked shiftily over his shoulder. 'I don't know how you saw through my disguise,' he whispered. 'But you're dead right. I'm not really a clown. I'm an undercover conservationist. And I'm on a secret mission of vital importance to the animal kingdom. If I don't succeed, an entire species will be wiped off the face of the planet!'

'Just run that by me again,' said Smiler. 'I don't think I quite got it the first time.'

Coriander glanced over. Had she heard? Smiler thought, suddenly. Did *she* understand first time? But her face had gone back to stone, so there was no way of telling.

Chapter Six

'Where's Coriander?' asked Smiler. He and Grandad were sitting in the fort's grey metal kitchen having a suppertime snack of baked beans and sausages.

'She says she's not hungry,' said Grandad, uneasily. 'She says she's having an early night. Have you seen her smile yet? Have you even seen the corners of her mouth crinkle?'

'Nope,' said Smiler, spooning up some beans.

Grandad shook his head, frowning. Bringing laughter back into Coriander's life was going to be a tough challenge.

Since Mr Funny Bones had made his amazing confession, Smiler hadn't paid much attention to Coriander. He had too many other things on his mind. He'd seriously considered telling Grandad that Laughter Club's clown was a fake, but somehow he couldn't bring himself to do it.

'You're not a sneak, Smiler,' he told himself. And besides, he was beginning to realize that he and Mr Funny Bones had quite a lot in common.

One last thing had convinced him not to tell. If Mr Funny Bones was on a secret mission, he, Smiler, didn't want to ruin it. Saving an entire species from extinction was really important work. Smiler wanted to know more about it.

'I've got to have a long talk with Mr Funny Bones,' decided Smiler.

But that was easier said than done. Mr Funny Bones was nowhere to be found. He was probably sneaking around those spooky corridors, where bright-green bunnies glowed and Giant Maggots did experiments with jellyfish.

Smiler shivered. He couldn't get the Maggot's hissing voice and piggy, eyeless face out of his head. He closed his fist round the limpet shell in his pocket. He had no evidence for it – it was only a gut feeling – but he was pretty sure the flute player was being held prisoner. And he wondered if the Giant Maggot was his jailer.

Grandad was still worrying about Coriander. 'Maybe tomorrow will be better,' he said.

'Why, what's the plan for tomorrow?' Smiler couldn't help asking. A plan would be a big comfort to his muddled mind.

'There's no plan!' said Grandad, shocked. 'We could kick off with a spot of Transcendental Chuckling. It works very well in India. They even imagine their *insides* smiling. You know, their gall bladder giggling, their colon chortling. That kind of thing.'

Smiler could picture Coriander's look of scorn. 'I already know she's not going to like that, Grandad,' warned Smiler, shaking his head.

'Well, what about chilling out with some Cloud Watching? That's always relaxing. It really frees up the mind.'

'Cloud watching's class,' agreed Smiler.

Just lying back and watching the clouds drift by. It was one of his favourite ways to waste time. You could see all kinds of shapes up there: camels, castles, killer whales.

'Maybe Coriander will like cloud watching,' said Grandad, only sounding half hopeful.

'Dream on, Grandad!' said Smiler, bitterly. 'She'll probably just say, "Cloud watching is for *children*!"'

Coriander wasn't in bed as Grandad believed. She was out on the landing stage. The tide was low. There was no water now, swirling around the fort's iron legs. Only a deep, dark pool underneath, where the conga eels lurked until the tide came in.

Seaweed fanned out over the pool's surface. It was silvery green in the moonlight.

It looks like a mermaid's hair, thought Coriander, hanging over the rail.

The music of the iron fort was clinking, tinkling, softly around her. The sound of the sea was just a distant *shushing*. Coriander found it all strangely soothing . . .

I could get to like Laughter Club, she surprised herself by thinking.

She felt herself suddenly *flopping*. It was so peaceful, no pressure . . .

Then she seemed to hear her dad's voice: 'A Jackson Never Wastes Time!' She stood stiffly to attention. She started to do her thirteen times table, in Mandarin, in her head. She worried, Why didn't I bring my mandolin? I need to practise those exam pieces!

Smiler licked the last of the tomato sauce off his knife. He pushed his plate away. He was at his wits' end with all these mysteries. He decided to put Grandad on the spot.

'You know that bright-green bunny that hops around this place?'

'Pardon?' said Grandad, staring at Smiler as if he were crazy. 'Oh, I get it, this is one of your jokes, right?'

Typical! thought Smiler. Why did no one *ever* take him seriously?

'This isn't a joke, Grandad,' Smiler insisted, clenching his fists in frustration. 'A joke is like, "What's brown and sticky?"'

On second thoughts, he wished he'd never brought that up.

He tried another question. 'What about that sign I saw in one of the corridors?'

HEALTH HAZARD!
NO PEOPLE BEYOND THIS POINT!

This time he'd hit the jackpot. 'You shouldn't be on that side of the fort,' said Grandad, sounding rattled. 'Someone else lives there.'

'I know that,' said Smiler. 'So why didn't you tell me?'

'I was going to,' Grandad replied, guiltily. 'When I had time. Anyway, I had to rent out part of the fort. Just to help me pay the bills. You've no idea how expensive it's been, getting Laughter Club off the ground –'

'Yes, yes, Grandad,' interrupted Smiler, impatiently. 'But why did you rent it out to someone so freaky? They look like a giant maggot, sort of crossed with a pig.'

'So you've seen her!' said Grandad, surprised. 'That protective suit she wears is a bit sinister.'

'Protective suit?' gaped Smiler. 'You mean there's a person *inside* there?' Why hadn't he realized that?

'Course,' said Grandad. 'It's Dr Maudlin. A lady about my age.'

Smiler groaned: 'Only an old lady?' He felt like a fool now for being so frightened.

'But how can she see and breathe?' asked Smiler. 'That black mask covers her face.'

'She breathes through the filter in the snouty bit. And that black mask is like mirrored sunglasses. You can't see her, but she can see you.'

'Oh, right,' nodded Smiler, smacking his forehead as if to say, 'How could I be so stupid?'

'I don't know why she needs all that safety gear,' added Grandad, who seemed to be pursuing his own thoughts. 'Or puts up that sign. It's all a bit over the top if you ask me. I mean, it's not like she's doing anything *dangerous* – I couldn't have children in this fort if she was. She's only studying jellyfish.'

'So she's, like, quite *normal,* is she then, Grandad?' Smiler was too relieved to hear the unease in Grandad's voice. 'She's not even a little bit creepy?'

'I didn't say that,' Grandad answered carefully.

His tenant had arrived under cover of night. He'd spotted her once in the metal corridors. She'd been wearing her safety suit. He'd shouted a cheery greeting: 'Good morning! Dr Maudlin, I presume!' She'd snorted something that sounded unfriendly, then strode off into the shadows.

'She's not very sociable,' said Grandad, tactfully.

He didn't want to bad-mouth his tenant. He needed her money too much – Laughter Club might go bust before it even got started. But, like Smiler said, she gave him the creepiest feeling. Why was she so secretive? Why all the safety precautions? He'd begun to wonder just what she was up to in her part of the fort.

Smiler missed the look of dark doubt in Grandad's eyes. In his own mind, he'd already written off Dr Maudlin as a harmless old boffin. Maybe a bit batty, but he could cope with that.

Smiler's mind was already rushing on to other questions. Where did head lice fit into all this? (Without thinking, he started scratching.) And what about fluorescent rabbits and flute players?

I need to find Mr Funny Bones, thought Smiler.

Still scratching, he wandered out on to the landing stage. He saw Coriander, playing air mandolin, practising her exam pieces.

Oh no, she's here, he thought, his heart sinking. If she'd been a different person, more matey, they might have shared a few jokes. He might even have shown her those strange fossil footprints in the rock.

Smiler sighed. It was no use wishing. The first member of Laughter Club was a smug, stuck-up little prig, a pain in the neck. The kind of kid he just couldn't stand.

Bet her life is just *perfect*! thought Smiler. Bet she *never* has any problems.

He ignored her and hurried off to find Mr Funny Bones. It was about time the fake clown gave him some answers.

Chapter Seven

Smiler plunged into the gloomy corridors. The luminous rabbit lolloped round a corner towards him.

This time, Smiler didn't do a double-take. Or smite his forehead and cry, 'A green glowing rabbit! I'm going crazy!' He just accepted it as part of the scenery.

'That's what this iron fort does to you,' he groaned.

He knelt down and stretched out his hand. He made encouraging clucking sounds. 'Come here! Come here!' he coaxed the rabbit.

But it just twitched its nose at him. Then turned round and hopped off on its own business. It seemed quite at home. Soon, it had shrunk to the size of a twinkling Christmas tree light.

Smiler was wondering whether to follow it, when he was surprised by a familiar sound.

'The flute!' he gasped.

Its music called to him through the grey metal tunnels.

'I'm going to free that flute player,' he told himself. 'And that Giant Maggot better not get in my way!'

He tried not to think of the snorting voice, the sinister, eyeless face.

'Inside that suit, there's just some wrinkly old jellyfish expert,' he reassured himself.

Then, a panicky voice suddenly shrilled inside his head: 'You've left your joke book behind again! It's under your pillow!'

How could he have done that? He used to take it everywhere with him. He didn't feel confident facing life without it.

But, to his own surprise, Smiler didn't go to pieces. He didn't rush back to get his book. Instead, he shook off that vulnerable feeling.

'Forget that old joke book,' he told himself, sternly. 'You don't need it.'

Smiler strode forward, into the tunnels, while the flute player piped his sad song.

Smiler touched the limpet shell in his pocket. Ran his thumb round its pearly insides, felt those strange, drilled holes.

The flute stopped. But it didn't matter. Smiler knew now just where it was coming from. He had a picture of that grim, bolted door in his head. He ignored the **NO PEOPLE BEYOND THIS POINT!** warning, then turned the last corner.

'Mr Funny Bones!'

He should have known he'd find the clown lurking down here, squinting sideways through the porthole of the jellyfish lab.

Mr Funny Bones didn't seem surprised to see Smiler. He even seemed to be expecting him. As if he took it for granted they were working together now.

'I've got to get in there,' he whispered. 'That's where she's hatching her evil plan. To wipe out an entire species!'

Moisture from his palms pinged softly on to the metal floor. What's he so worried about? wondered Smiler. This Dr Maudlin is just some crumbly old boffin.

'Exactly what species are you saving?' Smiler asked him.

Even though he was whispering, the fort snatched his voice and bounced it around the metal walls.

'Didn't I mention it before?' asked Mr Funny Bones, his frizzy orange clown wig shaking with enthusiasm. 'It's head lice.'

'Head lice!' cried Smiler, scornfully. This time, his voice rang through the fort like a gong. '*Head lice! Head lice!*'

What's he saving *them* for? wondered Smiler.

He'd naturally assumed Mr Funny Bones was on a secret mission to save something big and popular. Like giant tortoises from the Galapagos Islands or mountain gorillas. Saving *head lice*? Everyone hated them. It was like saving slugs or wasps.

'Dr Maudlin has dedicated her life to nits,' continued Mr Funny Bones, dramatically, 'but not to their welfare. She wants to destroy them! She's got some kind of fiendish plot.'

'So?' shrugged Smiler. '*Everyone* wants to destroy head lice. Mums get really worked up about them.'

His own mum nearly had a nervous breakdown last time he showed her one of those Nit Alert! notes from school. She hated them. Head lice were right at the top of her hit list.

'But what if it was pandas?' pleaded Mr Funny Bones. 'Or red squirrels? Everyone would be protesting!'

'The Doc would be doing the world a favour if she got rid of head lice,' insisted Smiler.

He felt cheated. He'd almost convinced himself Mr Funny Bones was some kind of hero. Now he suspected he was just barking mad.

Anyway, he hadn't come here to discuss head lice. He started walking towards the locked door.

'I'm gonna let that flute player out,' he said. 'Will you help me shift these bolts?'

Mr Funny Bones was still twittering behind him.

'But it's a *privilege* to get them! Just think! Your head becomes a miniature planet. With its own population of head lice. Hundreds of them! Getting on with their busy little lives. Dying, having babies. Sucking a bit of your blood. Grazing like tiny cows on your dandruff and dead skin –'

'I don't want to hear!' warned Smiler.

Those bolts were rusty. They didn't look as if they'd been opened since the First World War. How did the flute player get in there?

'All mammals get lice!' cried Mr Funny Bones, in a frantic attempt to convert Smiler. It was lonely being in a fan club of one. 'Except duck-billed platypuses,' he added. He made it sound as if duck-billed platypuses got a really raw deal.

'I don't *care* about head lice! OK?' said Smiler, exasperated.

He turned his attention back to the bolts. Freeing the flute player was going to be more difficult than he thought.

'Just imagine they're pandas –' Mr Funny Bones begged.

'*Shhhhh!*' Smiler held up his hand for silence. 'What's that sound?'

But he knew what it was already.

'*Sssssssssssss!*'

Smiler shivered. Why did he feel like running? 'Grow up!' he told himself. 'It's not a monster, right? It's only a wrinkly inside a safety suit!'

'Hide!' Mr Funny Bones hissed suddenly,

right in his ear. Smiler scuttled after him, round a corner.

He peeped out. Nothing moved. Except the jellyfish that he could see through the porthole. They fluttered in their tanks like strange, jewelled birds.

Clang! Smiler's heart gave a sick lurch. The door to the lab was open. The Suit stomped through first. It looked like an alien invader. It seemed to be even bigger than before. It swelled to fill the whole doorway! Despite himself, Smiler felt scared all over again. That baggy white skin, that sinister black snout. It was hard to imagine anything human inside it.

'*Sssssss!*' The Suit turned round to speak to someone behind it. It gasped and gurgled something.

'What's she saying?' hissed Smiler. 'I can't make it out.'

Mr Funny Bones seemed to know right away. 'She's saying,' he told Smiler, '"*Something nasty happened to me when I was a little girl.*"'

Of course, Smiler opened his mouth to whisper, 'What was it?' But the question was driven clean out of his head. Because he'd just seen the person she was talking to. And even more shocking than that, he'd just smelled him.

The smell was a reeking, rotting-fish stink. It made your eyes water.

'*Phew!*' Even Mr Funny Bones covered his red clown hooter with a clammy hand.

'It's him!' thought Smiler. He'd seen the figure which was shambling behind the Suit before. He'd seen it climbing the ladder, two weeks ago, on the night of the storm. When the fort had been a blue crackling fireball of electric energy.

'What's going on?' said Mr Funny Bones, shuffling forward to peer through the gloom.

'Feet!' mouthed Smiler, pointing urgently down.

Quickly, Mr Funny Bones pulled back the sticking-out toes of his green spotty shoes.

'*Sssssssss?*'

The great head of the Suit, white and wrinkly like a badly wrapped mummy, turned round slowly. Smiler and Mr Funny Bones shrank back. Had Dr Maudlin heard them?

She listened for a while, then plodded on.

She passed so close to their hiding place, they could have reached out and touched her. That choking fishy stench grew even stronger.

'Crikey!' said Mr Funny Bones, before Smiler crammed a hand over his mouth.

Her follower, a boy – as far as they could tell – turned to look at them. Was he really human? Smiler's breath seemed to freeze in his lungs. Would he give them away? The boy peered at them through shaggy hair.

What a freaky-looking kid! Smiler couldn't help thinking.

The face Smiler was staring at was like some crude modelling job. As if a toddler's thumbs had pressed it out of Play Doh. His nose was a big blob. His nostrils had extra-wide holes that seemed specially designed to suck up great hooterfuls of air. His brows stuck out like car bumpers. Beneath them, dull piggy eyes gazed at them.

He was wearing the weirdest clothes – a strange, rubbery black tunic. Smiler wondered, briefly, what it was made of. Then he noticed something far more important. The boy had a leather belt, and stuck into it was a white bone drilled with holes.

It's my flute player! thought Smiler. She's let him out. There must be another door to his prison, inside the lab.

Round the flute player's throat was a necklace of limpet shells on a string. Smiler could even see the space where his own shell had been.

Smiler didn't want to alert Dr Maudlin by speaking. Yet he longed to make contact. He had a sudden idea. He dug in his pocket and held up the single shell. He pointed to himself. Then pointed to the boy, as if to say, 'We're on the same side.' Did the strange, wild child understand?

The flute player seemed to come alive. His eyes changed from dull to bright. He started making noises, very softly – chirruping, twittering, low grunts. Was it some kind of language? He was *definitely* trying to tell them something. His hands made excited gestures, too quick for them to follow. Different expressions chased across his face, like clouds and sunshine.

'*Sssssss!*' A menacing snort came from down the corridor.

Smiler tried to shut the flute player up. He put his fingers to his lips: '*Shhhh!*'

'She's coming back!' Mr Funny Bones panicked, his flappy palms slippery with sweat. He knew a lot more about Dr Maudlin than Smiler or Grandad did. Only a fool wouldn't be afraid. 'She'll see us!'

The boy saved them. Before Dr Maudlin could come back and investigate, he waddled off to join her. Why was he walking like that? Were his shoes hurting him? They seemed to be woven out of straw.

What rubbish shoes, thought Smiler. What shop did he buy those from?

Long after the flute player had gone, his stink hung in the air. It smelled like 'dead crabs, left to rot in the midday sun.

Smiler and Mr Funny Bones stared at each other, speechless, for what seemed like ages.

Mr Funny Bones risked poking his red clown nose round the corner. 'It's OK. They've gone.'

At last, Smiler found some words. 'Where'd she find *him*?' he gasped.

Was he Dr Maudlin's goblin apprentice? Maybe some kind of troll, who lived in the fort's dark tunnels? It wouldn't surprise

Smiler. These tunnels were teeming with things you didn't expect. Scientists in safety suits, green glowing rabbits –

Anyway, decided Smiler, where he comes from doesn't matter now. The main thing is, we've got to save him. We've got to get him away from *her*.

Smiler felt all churned up inside. The sight of the poor, half-savage flute player had really distressed him.

He looks like an orphan boy that's been brought up by wolves, thought Smiler. Who's never had a mum to buy him deodorant. Or trendy trainers.

'You see the state of that kid?' Smiler asked Mr Funny Bones, in an outraged voice. 'It's child cruelty! I'd pay out of my *own* money for him to get a good haircut! It looks like he's dressed in a dustbin bag. And what about all that limpet-shell jewellery? He'll just get laughed at! Maybe he was brought up by limpets! That'd explain the smell. And limpets are probably useless parents . . .'

Smiler stopped himself, suddenly. 'I'm just talking a load of old rubbish, aren't I?' he apologized.

He gave his forehead a good *thwack* to knock some sense into it.

'I always say silly things when I'm upset,' he tried to explain to Mr Funny Bones.

But Mr Funny Bones wasn't listening. The wild goblin child would have to wait until later. He had something else to see to first.

He took a sneaky, spy-like glance over his shoulder. He wrung out his soggy hands. 'She didn't lock the door,' he told Smiler in a shaky whisper. 'You follow the flute player. I'm going to have a look in that lab.'

Mr Funny Bones took a few, fluttery breaths. The entire world population of head lice depends on you! he reminded himself. Then he flapped off, in his green and pink spotty shoes.

Smiler stared after him. He wouldn't fancy going on his own into Dr Maudlin's den.

You've got to admire that Mr Funny Bones, he was thinking. For a naturally nervous person, he was being really brave.

'Take care!' he called, as the clown went into the lab. Smiler had a quick glimpse of jellyfish lights fizzing like green fire. Then

Mr Funny Bones clanged the metal door shut behind him.

Chapter Eight

Smiler followed Dr Maudlin and the flute player. His face was grim. He was sure that the strange, primitive child was Dr Maudlin's prisoner. Even though she hadn't got him in handcuffs. She was driving him in front of her now, like a wild animal. He couldn't go fast, walking with that clumsy waddle.

It made Smiler really mad, but he didn't dare shout out.

'Leave him alone,' he murmured, under his breath. 'Stop pushing him, you bully.'

A green glow hopped by in the distance. Smiler hardly raised an eyebrow. He was getting used to the weird population that roamed these gloomy passages. He just thought, It's that rabbit again. Hadn't he got a hutch to go to?

Dr Maudlin clomped ahead. The spooky yellow light made her look even more like a mummy out of a horror film. '*Sssss! Sssss!*' That sinister, gasping breath didn't help.

Smiler's legs were shaking. And he already knew there was a person inside that suit! Did the flute player know this? If not, he must think he'd been kidnapped by some kind of hideous monster.

They passed Grandad's bedroom. Smiler pressed his ear against the metal door. He could hear snoring.

Good, thought Smiler. Grandad was safely asleep. Grandad had enough to worry about with Laughter Club. Smiler didn't want to give him any more problems.

They're going outside, thought Smiler, as Dr Maudlin nudged the flute player through the door that led to the landing stage.

Smiler hung back. Then opened the door a crack. He peered out. The landing stage was empty. That meant only one thing.

'They've gone down the ladder!'

Smiler crept after them. The sea was still far out. Mud flats, made silver by moonlight, stretched for miles.

'They're under the fort,' hissed a voice, right in Smiler's ear.

Smiler's heart almost stopped. His whole body froze. He creaked his neck stiffly round.

'Coriander!' He'd forgotten Little Miss Frosty Face. 'Where'd you come from?'

She gave a toss of her head. 'I was hiding in that old lifeboat,' she informed him.

Smiler felt like saying, 'Get lost! It's none of your business. Me and Mr Funny Bones can deal with this.'

But he knew he mustn't be rude to Coriander. Her parents had paid Grandad money.

You'd better get used to it, Smiler warned himself. If Laughter Club caught on, boatloads of kids like Coriander would be coming to the fort every week. Would a dose of laughter make any difference? Smiler doubted it. He didn't have faith in laughter any more, like Grandad did.

'Who are those two?' demanded Coriander. 'Are they members of Laughter Club?'

'You must be joking,' said Smiler.

'So who are they then?'

Better tell her, thought Smiler, or she'll make a big fuss.

'It's Dr Maudlin,' he whispered. 'She's the one in the safety suit. She rents a bit of the fort from Grandad to do her research.'

'But that smelly thing with her? What is it?' Coriander wasn't going to give up. *A Jackson never gives up!* That was a family saying.

'It's the flute player,' hissed Smiler, wishing she'd just stay out of his life.

'What grade in flute playing has he got?' asked Coriander immediately. 'Has he passed Grade Two?'

'*Shhh*, they'll hear you.' It wasn't likely. The wind and the clinking music of the metal fort covered up their voices, but Smiler just wanted Coriander to stop talking.

Carefully, so he didn't clang, Smiler sank to his knees, then spread himself out on the landing stage. He plugged his eye to a gap in the iron plates. He could see everything. 'Hey, they're down there.'

'I just told you that,' said Coriander. Secretly, she wondered if Smiler might be a little bit dumb. She'd heard there were kids like that. But her parents didn't let her mix with them.

What were Dr Maudlin and the flute player doing?

Smiler wriggled to get a better view. They were standing on the toffee-coloured rock. They were just beside the fossil footprints. But they didn't pay them any attention. A couple of metres behind them, the conger-eel pool glinted darkly.

Smiler hadn't noticed it before, but the flute player had a leather pouch on his belt. He opened it and put away his bone flute. He took out something else.

'I don't believe it!' hissed a voice into Smiler's ear.

Coriander was kneeling right beside him. Like him, she was goggling through a crack in the landing-stage floor. And, to Smiler's surprise, she'd swapped her stony expression for a look of wonderment.

'He's got a limpet spoon!' whispered Coriander, in an awed voice.

While Dr Maudlin watched, the flute player waddled over to one of the fort's iron legs, where limpets clustered in hundreds.

He used the sharp end of his spoon to rip one of them off, then the scoopy end to dig out its fishy insides. He tipped back his head.

'Did you hear what I said? It's a *limpet* spoon,' repeated Coriander, as if she expected Smiler to be as stunned as she was. 'You know, carved out of stone, specially for scoffing limpets,' she added, in case Smiler had missed the point.

Smiler looked baffled. Limpet spoons? What was she *talking* about? Whatever the point was, he'd missed it by miles.

'*Mmmmm!*' The flute player smacked his lips as the limpet slid down his throat.

'*Ughh!*' Smiler shuddered. 'That limpet was still alive!'

The flute player gobbled more and more live limpets. He kept looking around, like a dog at its food bowl, as if he expected someone to steal his dinner.

Wow, thought Smiler. He eats even faster than I do!

He was quick as lightning with that special spoon. *Rip, scoop, rip, scoop.* Soon piles of empty shells were scattered around his shoes.

The flute player took a rest from shovelling down limpets. He held his fat little belly and belched loudly. He scratched his bum. Even by Smiler's standards, his mealtime manners were a bit rough and ready.

An impatient snort came out of Dr Maudlin's mask. It meant, 'Dinnertime's over!'

The flute player shot her a scared look from under his ratty hair. He let the limpet he was chewing slither down. Then, sadly, he packed away his limpet spoon.

'It all fits,' whispered Coriander. 'There's loads of evidence. For a start, his shoes are plaited out of sand-dune grass. Next, he's got a sealskin tunic. The fur's on the inside,' Coriander pointed out fussily, 'to keep him extra warm. *Then* there's his limpet spoon. But it's his *occipital bun* that makes me really sure.'

'Pardon?' said Smiler, who'd been feeling for some time that he'd totally lost the plot.

'*Occipital bun*,' repeated Coriander, with a tiny sigh at Smiler's stupidity. 'That bony bulge on the back of his skull. You can't fake that.'

Smiler stared at her. He hardly dared hope. '*Are you telling me you know who he is?*'

'I know *what* he is,' said Coriander. 'He's one of the Limpet People, who used to live along this coast.'

'But I've never *heard* of these Limpet People,' protested Smiler.

'Of course not,' said Coriander. 'You haven't been to after-school *Advanced* Archaeology classes, like me. Anyway, the Limpet People were Neanderthals.'

Smiler could only repeat, numbly, '*Neanderthals?*'

'And as even you must know,' added Coriander, 'Neanderthals have been extinct for thirty thousand years.'

Chapter Nine

Once he was inside Dr Maudlin's lab, Mr Funny Bones switched the lights off. But he could still see. Other lights, green glowing ones, flickered from tanks all around him.

'Fluorescence!' muttered Mr Funny Bones.

He tiptoed around in the green gloom. There weren't only jellyfish. She'd collected all sorts of creatures that glowed. In one tank, tiny transparent rugby balls zipped about. You could only see where they were because of the twinkling lights inside them.

'Sea gooseberries,' murmured Mr Funny Bones to himself. He was so intrigued he forgot to feel scared. 'And what's in this tank?' He stood sideways and squinted into it.

Inside, squelchy, spongy stuff glowed with an eerie green light.

'Slime,' decided Mr Funny Bones. 'She's even got luminous slime mould from somewhere.'

The slime mould was made up of millions of microscopic one-celled animals. Mr Funny Bones didn't notice, but it was making an escape bid, slithering up the side of the tank. Soon it would reach the top.

So that's her little game, thought Mr Funny Bones, as he sneaked around the lab. He'd guessed what Dr Maudlin was up to, ever since he'd seen that glowing rabbit.

She'd been mucking about with the genes that make creatures light up, swapping them from one species to another.

It wasn't rocket science. These days, it was fairly routine stuff. They'd been breeding glowing mice, even glowing moths, in labs for a long time now. If you wanted them, you could get tomatoes that glowed green in the dark.

Mr Funny Bones would have bet a million pounds on what he was going to find next.

'Bingo!' he whispered, triumphantly.

He'd found another tank. It had some wispy cotton wool in the bottom. And along each white cotton-wool strand, clusters of tiny lights, smaller than pin pricks, sparkled.

Luminous nits! thought Mr Funny Bones.

You had to hand it to Dr Maudlin. Her plan was simple. But ingenious! Lice eggs that light up in the dark. Mr Funny Bones could imagine the headlines now:

DR MAUDLIN ENDS HEAD-LICE MENACE. PARENTS OVER THE MOON

Just turn out the lights and, hey presto, your kid's head will light up like Blackpool illuminations! It's a piece of cake to comb out those nasty nits –

'They're hatching out!' said Mr Funny Bones. They were too small to see clearly. But Mr Funny Bones knew they were popping out of those eggs like corks bursting from champagne bottles.

'*Awwwww,*' murmured Mr Funny Bones. 'The miracle of life!'

Each egg contained a tiny air bubble. The baby louse gulped in some air, then blasted it out of its bottom. This jet-propelled it – *whoosh* – into the Big Wide World.

What a speedy way to be born, thought Mr Funny Bones. If only human babies could do that. Though you'd probably have to catch them in a butterfly net.

'Concentrate!' Mr Funny Bones told himself sternly. He wasn't there to admire one of the marvels of nature.

Tiny, glittering insects scuttled off into the cotton wool. The baby lice were luminous too! With eggs *and* lice lit up, a kid's hair would be twinkling like a Christmas tree! There'd be no hiding place left for head lice. No escape from a mum's eagle eye. Soon they'd be nit-combed to extinction.

It's only a matter of time, thought Mr Funny Bones, tragically, before there is only *one* lonely head louse left on our planet. He felt a deep sense of injustice. They've got as much right to survive as pandas! They're part of life's rich pattern!

But Dr Maudlin had spent most of her life trying to wipe them out. She didn't do it for profit. It was personal. She must have a really big grudge against them. Mr Funny Bones had often wondered what it was. He knew something nasty had happened to her years ago. She was always going on about that. But she never, *ever*, spoke about the details.

Whatever happened to her, thought Mr Funny Bones, doesn't make this right. This is *wrong*! Tinkering about with a creature's genes. To make them easier to kill!

Nit combs broke their legs, so they couldn't cling to your hair. Without human dandruff to snack on, head lice would starve to death. Mr Funny Bones' kindly nature cringed at the thought.

It's cruel.

A world without head lice would be a poorer place. Surely everyone could see that?

But maybe sparkly hair might catch on! he tried to convince himself. Kids will think it's groovy. It'll look great at discos.

He knew it was useless to hope. Parents would cheer when they heard about Dr Maudlin's invention, but *someone* had to stand up for unpopular species.

'You alone,' Mr Funny Bones told himself, wringing out his soggy hands, 'can save the humble louse from being combed off the face of the earth.'

But there was still one thing Mr Funny Bones didn't understand. Dr Maudlin's evil plan of mass extermination would only work if every nit and head louse in the world lit up.

'It's impossible,' puzzled Mr Funny Bones. 'How's she going to arrange that?'

As if to answer his question, he heard a clattering behind him. It sounded like an angry rattlesnake.

Mr Funny Bones spun round on his spotty shoes. 'Who's there?' Then he saw where the noise was coming from.

Shut in a tank on its own was a glowing creature. What was it? It had claws and lots of legs. Its body looked armour-plated. And it was very, very annoyed. It kept whacking itself against the glass, desperate to get out.

Is it a little lobster? wondered Mr Funny Bones. Then he realized. His hands flapped about in horror. Those claws weren't for catching shrimps. They were for clinging on to hair.

'It's not a little lobster. It's a giant head louse!'

For a head louse it was huge – about the same size as a field mouse. It wasn't only fluorescence genes that Dr Maudlin had been fiddling with.

Rat, tat, tat, tat, tat.

Suddenly, from all sides, came the sound of claws furiously rapping on glass. It was as loud as machine-gun fire.

Mr Funny Bones whirled round. 'There are more of them!'

Lots, lots more – each glowing green in its own little tank. And each one in a very, very bad mood.

'What's she playing at?' gasped Mr Funny Bones. 'She's breeding giant, glowing head lice!'

And they were so fierce. Scuttling around, slashing at the air with their claws. They were fighting mad! Worse than a cornered scorpion.

What has she done to them? thought Mr Funny Bones.

Normal lice weren't as wild as this. They went about their daily lives, on your head, quite peacefully. They kept a low profile. If they weren't so itchy, you'd probably never know they were there.

Why had Dr Maudlin bred these scary superlice? What did she plan to do with them?

Surely, thought Mr Funny Bones, shuddering, she's not going to let them loose on kids' heads!

Chapter Ten

Out on the landing stage, Smiler was still gob-smacked.

'Are you *serious*?' he hissed softly. 'He's nothing like a Neanderthal. They wore furs and hunted woolly mammoths with spears. They were really fierce. Everyone knows that.'

'Well, everyone's wrong,' Coriander corrected him. 'The Limpet People were peaceful and gentle.'

'And they actually lived around here?'

'Right where this fort is now,' whispered Coriander. 'Archaeologists have dug up loads of their limpet spoons. Surely you've seen them in the museum?'

Smiler didn't like to admit that he'd never once been to the museum – to see limpet spoons, or anything else. He'd probably been wasting his time cloud watching.

'Course,' Coriander continued, 'the coastline has changed since then. Thousands of years ago this was dry land.'

'But if he's Neanderthal,' Smiler said, his mind boggling, 'how'd he end up here? In the twenty-first century?'

Their eyes met for a second. Smiler was startled to see that Coriander looked as clueless as he was.

The wind was getting brisker. Metal was clinking madly all around them. Smiler could hear a low rumbling sound in the distance. The tide was coming back in. Dr Maudlin and the flute player wouldn't be able to stay down there for much longer.

'Let's see what they're doing now,' suggested Coriander.

They both spied again through the gaps in the metal plates.

The space under the fort was a tangle of moonlight and shadows. The boy had finished his dinner of limpets. Now he wanted pudding. His play-dough face became like a pleading puppy's. He pointed to the conger-eel pool.

Dr Maudlin loomed over him. She looked like a ghostly monster in the gloom. Her breath came gasping through her mask, '*Rrrrrrrrrrrr.*' Then she gurgled something.

They seemed to understand each other. The boy gave a grunt of delight. He untied his grassy shoes. He happened to be standing in a puddle of silver moonlight.

'Look at his bare feet!' whispered Coriander. Her voice sounded thunderstruck. Smiler saw why.

He had flipper feet, webbed, like a frog's.

The fossil footprints! Smiler thought straight away. He couldn't see them, but they were there in the rock, not far from where the boy was standing.

But there was no time now to think about fossils. Not when he had what *might* be a real live Neanderthal to watch. Smiler stared, fascinated, as the boy pulled something out of his leather pouch.

'It's a net.'

'Woven out of sand-dune grass, probably,' said Coriander, right into his ear. 'The Limpet People used that for loads of things. Baskets, shoes, house roofs –'

'He's going into the pool!' hissed Smiler excitedly.

Now they knew why he was clumsy on land. Feet like that weren't built for walking, but in water they worked like a dream. While Dr Maudlin watched, the boy did a perfect dive. Then twisted and turned like a dolphin in the pool. His webbed feet flickered. He dived, clutching the net. He was down for ages.

'He'll drown!' said Smiler.

But Limpet People could swim before they could walk. The sea was where they loved to be. Bubbles fizzed up, then a head, sleek and black, broke the surface.

'It's him!' whispered Smiler, as the head disappeared again. 'He looks like a seal. Seal's a good nickname for him. What do you think?'

He could have kicked himself for asking Coriander. She would only say, in that smarty-pants voice that made him feel so small and silly, 'Nicknames are for *children*.'

Instead she surprised him with a question, 'You *sure* there's no exam at the end of Laughter Club?' She didn't sound smug. She sounded quite panicky.

'No,' frowned Smiler. What did she want to know about that for *now*? 'There are no tests at all. Laughter Club's not like school.'

'Because, if there *is* an exam,' fretted Coriander. 'I *definitely* won't come top. *I might even fail it,*' she whispered, as if that would be *unthinkable*. 'I don't know any answers! What are the rules in this place? I don't know what's going on.'

'Me neither,' said Smiler, who was more used to not knowing answers than Coriander. 'But don't freak out. The iron fort's like that. It's like nowhere else you've ever been.'

Was that his own voice? It sounded so wise, so confident! Hey, you didn't sound silly at all there, Smiler, he thought, amazed.

He peered down again at the pool. 'Seal's coming up. He's caught a conger eel!'

The eel was thrashing about in Seal's net, writhing itself into slimy knots. It was almost as long as he was. But Seal didn't flinch. He climbed out of the dark pool, lugging it after him. *Whop!* He whacked it on a rock. He whacked it again. The eel twitched, then lay still.

Seal smacked his lips. He started untangling the eel from the net.

He's not going to eat it raw! thought Smiler, feeling sick. Oh, yes he is!

Then just as Seal opened his mouth to tear off a chunk, Dr Maudlin tipped her big, mummy's head to one side. She seemed to be listening.

'*Shhhh!*' Coriander and Smiler warned each other.

But she wasn't listening to them. She'd heard the roaring of the waves, coming closer. She knew they hadn't much time.

'*Sssss, rrrrrrrr.*'

Her robot voice ordered Seal back to the ladder. He slung his conger eel over his shoulder like a fire hose. She shoved him, just in case he hadn't got the message. Seal, so graceful in water but so awkward on land, waddled over the rock with his froggy, webbed feet.

'Leave him alone!' shouted Smiler angrily. 'Let him put his shoes on!'

The wind, getting wilder and wilder, whisked away his words. She couldn't possibly have heard him, but Dr Maudlin stopped shoving. She waited while Seal unloaded the floppy eel, then tied on his dune-grass shoes. He squatted down to pick up his night-time snack.

An order roared out. The mask amplified it like a stereo speaker.

'LEAVE IT!' thundered Dr Maudlin as if Seal was a dog who'd found something disgusting. She jabbed her gloved hand at the rock. '*SSSSSSSSSS. PUT IT DOWN!*'

Her words were even louder than the sea.

Seal trembled with fear. She seemed, to him, like a great bellowing monster. But he understood what she was telling him. His rubbery face turned tragic. After one last look at his catch, he turned away.

To comfort himself, his hand shot out and snatched a big daddy-long-legs that was flying by. Seal crammed it into his mouth. Its legs were still kicking.

'More proof,' said Coriander. 'Eating insects was part of the Neanderthal diet. They're very nutritious –'

'Come on!' Smiler yanked at her arm. 'They're climbing the ladder. We've got to get out of here.'

Then a terrible thought flashed through his brain: I bet she goes straight back to the lab.

'Quick,' he screamed into Coriander's ear. 'We've got to warn Mr Funny Bones!'

Chapter Eleven

Mr Funny Bones had forgotten he was only supposed to be sneaking a quick look in the lab. He was sitting at a bench, his red nose buried in Dr Maudlin's notes. Beside him, one of the glowing superlice glared from its glass tank. It was the same size as a cute little mouse, but it had the fighting instincts of a rattlesnake.

Rat-a-tat-a-tat. Its claws clattered on the sides of its glass prison. They were small but razor sharp. Before he read on, Mr Funny Bones checked the tank lid was tightly shut.

'My plan became possible,' Dr Maudlin wrote, 'when, by sheer chance, I got a fresh supply of head lice.'

Where from? wondered Mr Funny Bones. But her notes didn't tell him that.

'They are a type unknown to science,' continued Dr Maudlin. 'They are already naturally aggressive –'

'She's right about that,' shivered Mr Funny Bones.

'– and with the addition of jellyfish genes and growth hormones, they will be perfect for my plans.'

Clunk!

The head louse near his elbow had spotted another head louse further down the bench. Both of them went berserk – hurling themselves against the tank sides, trying to get at each other!

Hope that glass holds out, thought Mr Funny Bones.

'They will not attack humans,' Dr Maudlin's notes told him.

Phew! thought Mr Funny Bones, wiping his damp hands on his baggy clown trousers. Thank goodness for that.

'But the males will instantly fight off any rival male head louse. They will defend their territory, that is, a human head, to the death,' wrote Dr Maudlin in her nice, neat handwriting.

Eh? thought Mr Funny Bones. He read feverishly on.

As her plan became clear, Mr Funny Bones didn't know whether to be impressed or appalled.

'It's so beautifully simple!' he couldn't help murmuring.

Smiler came rushing in. Coriander was at his side.

'She's on her way back!' gasped Smiler. Seal's clumsy walk meant Dr Maudlin was making slow progress. She was a long way behind them. 'Don't panic though,' said Smiler. 'You've got a few minutes.'

But Mr Funny Bones didn't go into a flap or wring out his sweaty palms. He looked up, dazed, as if he hadn't even heard Smiler speak.

'What are these giant, luminous cockroach things?' asked Coriander.

Mr Funny Bones told them everything. He talked about Dr Maudlin's experiments. He mentioned the fluorescent rabbit.

'Fluorescent rabbit?' said Coriander, raising her eyebrows.

'Yes, but you can forget about that,' said

Mr Funny Bones. 'It isn't a major part of the plot.'

Smiler listened in growing horror as Mr Funny Bones explained what he'd read in Dr Maudlin's notes.

'Are you kidding me? You mean, Dr Maudlin's going to let them loose? A kid could have one of those giant insects squatting on his head? What are they going to be doing up there?'

'Acting like they own the place,' said Mr Funny Bones, still looking stunned. 'Fighting off all the male head lice. Then mating with the females. The eggs and baby head lice that are born will be luminous, just like their dad. Then along comes a sharp-eyed human with a nit comb –' Mr Funny Bones shuddered. 'Soon head lice will be history.'

'Wait a minute!' yelled Smiler. 'What about us poor kids? Walking around with Insect Wars on our heads. Not to mention the other disgusting stuff going on up there.' Smiler cringed just thinking about it.

'What d'you mean, using your head as a toilet?'

'*Yuk!*' Smiler squirmed more than ever.

'What did you tell me that for?'

'Oh, you mean *mating*!' said Mr Funny Bones, consulting Dr Maudlin's notes. 'They do a lot of that. If they're not fighting, they're mating, it says here. They're very macho. And, isn't this fascinating, they flash on and off to attract females. Apparently, lady head lice just can't resist it –'

'*Aaaargh!* I don't want to know that either!' yelled Smiler, covering his ears.

'It's just biology,' said Mr Funny Bones.

'It's *embarrassing*! What if it starts flashing on and off? All your mates'll be sniggering, "We know what's going on on your head!"'

Coriander was trying to cope with lots of new feelings. Smiler was right. The iron fort was like nowhere she'd ever been. It was full of mysteries she didn't know the answer to. That scared her. But she'd just made the strangest discovery. It was exciting too. Like being on a roller-coaster ride.

Her brain was buzzing with questions. 'Won't these superlice get combed out with all the rest?' she wanted to know.

'*Hummm,*' said Mr Funny Bones. 'You'd have to have a pretty big nit comb. I don't know where Dr Maudlin found them, but we're talking about head lice with attitude here.'

'I'd soon get rid of it!' shouted Smiler. 'If it was sitting up there on *my* head, I'd whack it with a big stick!'

He instantly thought, Oh no, I'd just bash my own brains in! *Why* do I say such stupid things?

He prepared to feel small. He just knew Coriander was going to say something cutting.

But, to his surprise, she didn't even raise an eyebrow. And Mr Funny Bones, of course, was too kind to point out the flaw in his plan.

Instead he warned, 'They're not that easy to kill. They've got a body shell as hard as steel. And, if what Dr Maudlin says is true, once one of them has chosen your head, it'll never leave it. Not while it's still alive.'

'You mean, you're *stuck* with it?' interrupted Smiler, appalled.

''Fraid so,' said Mr Funny Bones.

'Oh, *great*,' groaned Smiler.

As if kids didn't have enough problems

these days! He had a nightmare vision of every kid in the playground permanently attached to their own personal parasite. Staring around like it was saying, 'This head is *mine*!' And what about the itchiness question? He'd hardly given that a thought. *Ordinary* head lice made you scratch like crazy. These superlice were bound to itch a million times more.

Coriander was nearest to the lab door. What was that strange, snorting sound echoing down the dark corridors?

'How long do these lice live?' Smiler asked Mr Funny Bones, hoping for some crumb of comfort.

'Ordinary head lice only live three weeks,' said Mr Funny Bones, 'but with these mutant lice bred in a laboratory . . . who knows?'

He started checking Dr Maudlin's notes to see if they gave him any clues.

Smiler was going off into fantasy land. What if they live for *years*? he thought, frantically. How am I *ever* gonna get a girlfriend? What chance would I have with a giant louse living on my head? Girls these days are dead picky. (His big brother had told him that.) And if she's got her own superlouse, how could I give her a kiss? We could never get close enough! Not without our superlice trying to fight to the death!

A voice behind him said, 'Hadn't we better hide? I mean, NOW!'

But Smiler was so busy fretting about his future love life that he didn't hear Coriander's warning.

It didn't matter. It came too late anyway.

The lab door was flung open.

'*Sssssss!*' A hooded, white figure loomed in the doorway. Where its face should be was nothing but black blankness. But you could tell it was angry. A gasping roar came out of the mask. 'WHAT – *ssssss* – IS GOING ON HERE?'

Mr Funny Bones sprang up. Then he slipped on something slimy. With his clown shoes leading the way, he did a spectacular somersault. As he came down, one of his long toes caught a superlouse tank. *Crash!* It shattered on the lab floor. Something glowing, like a green star, shot out of the broken glass. You could hear its tiny claws scraping on the floor.

'Cover your hair, kids!' cried Mr Funny Bones. 'It's vicious. And it's looking for a home!'

He wasn't in danger. He was wearing a frizzy orange wig. Dr Maudlin had her whole head hidden. But Smiler freaked out. '*Aaaargh!*' He pulled his T-shirt up and smothered his head. Even Coriander covered her hair with her hands.

Dr Maudlin moved fast. '*Sssss.*' She booted the lab door shut to cut off the giant insect's escape.

She should have known better. After all, she'd spent a lifetime studying them. A head louse has a sinister talent. When mums come after it with nit combs, it flattens itself next to your scalp so it's hard to scrape off. The superlouse simply squeezed itself thin as a penny. Then posted itself under the lab door.

'Oh no!' said Mr Funny Bones, flapping his hands in distress. It was just what he'd been trying to prevent. 'This is a disaster! A luminous louse is loose in the outside world!'

Smiler pulled his T-shirt back down over his skinny ribs. 'Has it gone?'

Someone started laughing.

It started as a giggle. '*Tee hee hee.*' Then became a chortle. Then a big rocking, roaring belly laugh. '*HO, HO, HO!*' It was the kind of sound that Grandad would have loved to hear, that Laughter Club was dreamed up for – but had failed to deliver, so far.

Everyone's head whipped round. Except Dr Maudlin, who had to turn her great, grim head more slowly.

'Seal!' said Coriander. 'When did you sneak in?' Had he been hidden under a bench?

'What are you laughing at?' Smiler asked him. This was crisis time. Laughing seemed like the last thing to do.

He went very close to the Neanderthal. Seal's fishy stink made his nose wrinkle.

Seal cringed back. The laughter in his eyes died. His little troll face peeped anxiously at Smiler through his salt-crusted hair.

'What are you laughing at?' asked Smiler again. 'You know, *laughing*?' He gave a few hearty *ho, ho, ho*s to show what he meant.

Seal pointed past Smiler.

'At *me*?' said Mr Funny Bones, the world's worst clown, in a disbelieving voice.

'Yeah, yeah!' said Smiler, excitedly. 'It must have been when you tripped up.'

'But I did that ages ago.'

'Maybe he only just got the joke. Remember, he's from the Stone Age. Go on,' urged Smiler. 'Do it again!'

For a second, it looked as if Mr Funny Bones was thinking about it. He was touched. Seal was the only child who had ever found him funny. But then he gave himself a serious shake.

'There's no time for clowning now!' He was surprised by how tough and determined his voice sounded. That fluttery feeling, like a thousand butterflies' wings beating inside him, had faded away. Thinking of wildlife in danger had made him strong.

'We've got to get that superlouse back,' he said. 'If even *one* escapes, it will be the end of head lice as we know them.'

Smiler didn't say, 'And a good job too.' He was thinking of other things, much more important to him than head lice.

But Coriander beat him to it. She faced up to Dr Maudlin and asked the very same questions that had been on the tip of Smiler's tongue.

'What about Seal? Why are you keeping him prisoner? He should be back with the Limpet People where he belongs. How did he get here in the first place? How –?'

But her urgent questions were interrupted.

'*Sssssss!*' Dr Maudlin ignored her. She turned her black mask towards Mr Funny Bones. 'By what right – *sssssssss* – do you interfere in my research?' that menacing voice snorted. 'Do I *know* you?'

Mr Funny Bones yanked off his red clown nose. Underneath, his own nose was sharp and quivering. He pulled off his frizzy orange wig. Smiler did a double-take. Beneath it, his own hair was almost the same. It was frizzy too, and the colour of carrots.

What did he bother wearing a wig for? thought Smiler, amazed.

Using his sleeve, Mr Funny Bones scrubbed off his chalk-white make-up.

He raised his head. Without his clown disguise he looked very young and vulnerable.

He walked up to Dr Maudlin and stared straight into the black mask. He couldn't see her. But he knew she could see him.

'Hello, Mother,' he said. 'It's your son, Dexter. Remember me?'

Chapter Twelve

Was Dr Maudlin surprised? Was she angry or pleased to see her son? You couldn't tell, under that protective suit, what she was feeling. You couldn't even tell if she was human.

She stood there for a few seconds, snorting quietly.

'I rebelled, Mother,' Dexter Maudlin was explaining. 'All your talk of killing creatures made me a conservationist. I'm quite well known now, in case you're interested, as a champion of small, unpopular species. I suspected you were hatching some new plot. And I'm here to stop you.'

The mask seemed to look at her son for a moment, then that great head swung away.

'*Sssss*. No time for chit-chat now. First

priority – *sssssssss* – get superlouse back.'

Her arms, as wrinkly as elephant skin, began sweeping the air. She was making signs to Seal, trying to drive him back into his prison.

Seal shuffled obediently across the lab. Everything about what had happened bewildered him. The way he'd somehow lost his Stone Age family and ended up here. The way the White Monster had hunted through his hair – and hadn't crunched his head lice between her teeth and eaten them, like his own mother would have done, but had kept them alive, even the biggest, juiciest ones! And taken them away somewhere.

She had even taken away his light, the luminous slime mould that he kept in his leather pouch. It was very scary, stuck in a cave, all on his own in the dark.

There was one thing Seal knew, though. He knew it would be the next low tide before he'd be let out for more food. She'd made him leave his eel behind. So, in each fist, he'd tucked two of his precious limpets for when he got hungry.

Smiler watched Seal trudge up to his

metal cell. Twin feelings of fury and disgust suddenly hit him. They were so powerful, it felt like someone had punched him.

'No way!' he cried, rushing to stand between Seal and the cell door.

'Prison cells are NOT for children,' said Coriander in her best smarty-pants voice. But this time Smiler didn't flinch because he knew she was on his side.

'You mustn't keep him here, Mother,' said Dexter, backing them up. 'Is he a late arrival for Laughter Club? Where did he come from?'

'The Stone Age,' said Coriander.

Dexter's eyes jiggled wildly as Coriander's words sunk in. 'You're joking!' he cried out. But joking wasn't Coriander's style.

'Go on, ask her. *Ask her* if he's one of the Limpet People,' urged Coriander.

A warning snarl came through Dr Maudlin's mask.

We're for it now! Smiler thought. It was three against one. Usually good odds, but not when you're up against an Incredible Hulk.

Suddenly the suit shrugged and turned

its back on them all, as if they weren't important to its plans. It stomped out of the door.

'Is that really your *mum*?' asked Smiler, his mouth sagging open.

'She's in there somewhere,' said Dexter, staring bleakly after Dr Maudlin.

'Don't think I'm being nosy or anything,' asked Smiler, 'but did she come dressed like that to parents' evenings?'

Dexter sighed. 'She never came at all. Something nasty happened to her when she was a girl. Since then, her crusade against head lice was all she *really* cared about. It broke our family up. Dad left. She sent me away to boarding school –'

Dexter stopped and gave himself a shake. 'But you don't want to listen to all that now. We've got to catch that mutant louse. For the sake of an entire species.'

'And for the sake of us kids!' Smiler reminded him. 'I don't want a superlouse swaggering around on *my* head! Acting like it owns the place!'

'What about Seal?' asked Coriander

Dexter's mind was still boggling about

that. 'He *can't* have come here through time. *Surely* there's another explanation?'

'Look at the back of his head,' said Coriander. 'You can't fake an occipital bun.'

Suddenly Smiler spoke. 'This iron fort,' he said. 'It's got lots of power.'

He was thinking about the night of the storm when the fort crackled with energy. When it drew all the lightning flashes in heaven to it like a giant magnet, then blazed in the night like a blue meteor.

'Those fossil footprints,' he said, trying to sort out his own thoughts, 'what if they're Seal's? What if, the night of the storm, but thirty thousand years ago, he was standing on that exact same spot, peacefully limpet collecting or something, and the fort sucked him through time? Like a sort of giant Hoover!'

Coriander didn't say, 'Giant Hoover? That's silly!' To his surprise, she took him seriously. Hardly anyone did that.

She repeated something she'd said before, out on the landing stage, 'I don't know the rules of this place.' She was getting used to that now. It didn't throw her into a panic any more, like it did when she first arrived. 'But what if even the rules of time can get broken?'

She and Smiler stared at each other, their eyes full of mystery and wonder.

Dexter said, 'It does *feel* like the kind of place where anything can happen.'

'*Yip, yip, yip, yip.*' Loud yelping noises broke their mood. It was Seal. He sounded like a scared puppy.

Since Dr Maudlin had gone, Seal had been staring anxiously from one to the other. He was thinking, Are my new owners going to hurt me? At least the White Monster had fed him. And let him swim.

Suddenly his fear became too great. He just couldn't control it.

'*Owwww! Owwww!*'

He threw back his shaggy head and howled. He seemed inconsolable. Shrimps and a few tiny crabs flew out of his hair. It nearly broke Smiler's heart to hear him.

'Make him laugh, Mr Funny Bones,' said Smiler, giving Dexter a nudge.

'What? Me?'

'Yeah, he really likes you.'

'What? *Me?*'

Dexter Maudlin could hardly believe it. He'd made a friend! He'd had a lonely childhood. It was a lonely life now, sticking up for small, unpopular species. People wouldn't support his Save a Slug campaign: gardeners wrote him hate mail. No one wanted to join his Be Kind to Cat Fleas Club. Or wear his I LOVE HEAD LICE badges.

Dexter started off with his trick bow tie. He made it twizzle. He made it twinkle: '*Ta da!*'

A puzzled frown crept on to Seal's tear-stained face. But he didn't smile.

'Fall over!' hissed Smiler. 'That worked before.'

'Mind out of my way, then.'

With a wild and reckless look in his eyes – *whoops!* – Mr Funny Bones tripped himself up. He did a loop-the-loop! His orange hair frizzed out round his head like a sunburst. He slid the length of the lab and ended up squashed in a corner like a concertina.

A jerky little smile tugged at the corners of Seal's mouth.

Dexter tried to get up. But his clown shoes got tangled. 'Oh no!' He went crashing down again. *Kerrak!* He head-butted a bench. 'Ow!'

That did it. Seal forgot his fear. His little eyes, under his car bumper brows, lit up. He chuckled. Then opened his mouth and roared with laughter. He staggered about. He held his belly as if it hurt.

'I think I've done my back in,' said Dexter, hobbling over to join them. 'And I might have fractured my skull.'

'Never mind that now,' said Smiler. 'You're a star!'

Dexter's eyes beamed with pride and pleasure. He'd been a complete failure with kids as Mr Funny Bones. But now a Stone Age child was his biggest fan.

'Come on,' Coriander reminded them. 'Let's get moving. That louse is getting away.'

The small group of hunters moved cautiously through the grey metal tunnels.

'Look on the ceilings and the walls,' warned Dexter.

'Can it climb?' asked Smiler, horrified. His eyes were flickering all over, trying to spot anything that glowed green and scuttled.

'I don't know,' admitted Dexter. 'It's a mutant. We're dealing with something completely unknown to science.'

Back in the lab, something else unknown to science was making its great escape. It had already slithered out of its glass prison. Now it was searching for food.

The slime mould that Dr Maudlin stole from Seal had been extinct on earth since the Ice Age. There are still luminous slime moulds around, but none that feeds on metal – and moves so fast. If Dr Maudlin hadn't been so obsessed with head lice, she might have found that out.

Back in the Stone Age, the slime mould chomped its way through metal ore found in the earth, but today was its birthday. It had never had so much to feed on. A whole metal fort to devour! Those tiny, slimy microbes soon got busy.

They munched a hole in the lab floor. Like a green glowing lava flow, they dropped through to the floor beneath. The more iron they ate, the more they multiplied. And the faster they moved.

Chapter Thirteen

Smiler desperately wanted to scratch.

'No!' he told himself. With all this talk of superlice, he'd raked his scalp red raw.

He wished there'd been time to have his head shaved. The thought of the giant louse, plopping from the darkness into his hair – fighting, mating, feasting on his dandruff – made him feel faint with horror.

How could I concentrate on my computer games, he thought. I'd never get a minute's peace!

'Careful,' said Coriander. 'It could be anywhere.' Even she seemed flustered.

It could be clinging to the lights. There were strings of them down each corridor, casting a dim yellow glow. It could have made itself thin as a cracker, then squeezed itself between the iron plates. It could be targeting their heads right NOW.

Smiler had lots of sympathy with Dr Maudlin's personal grudge against head lice. At this moment he loathed that superlouse like poison.

Then Dexter made a generous offer. 'Anyone want to cover their hair with my clown wig?' he asked. 'It might give you some protection.'

Coriander said, '*Errr*, no thanks. Think I'll take my chances.'

Seal grunted, 'Ugh?' He didn't understand. Anyway, it would never have fitted over his wild, shaggy hair.

'Smiler?' asked Dexter, holding out what looked like an extra-large helping of orange candy floss.

Smiler had a tough struggle with himself. Wearing a frizzy clown wig was totally uncool. Everyone knew that. But in the circumstances, who cared? He tugged it on.

'How do I look?' he couldn't help asking Coriander.

Were her lips curving into a banana

shape? Surely the frosty-faced Coriander couldn't be *smiling*?

Grandad's *never* going to believe this! thought Smiler. He'll be jumping for joy! He'll think Laughter Club really works.

But Smiler was mistaken. When he looked at Coriander again, her lips were straight as two sticks of celery.

'Knew it was too much of a miracle,' he sighed.

What was that scratchy sound?

'Louse alert!' hissed Dexter.

They all stopped dead and listened. Could that be claws scrabbling? Was that a sparkle of green light?

'It's there! NO, there!' cried Dexter

While they were dithering, Seal did something. He amazed them all. His reactions were instant. Quick as the flicker of a humming bird's wing, in one movement too fast for their eyes to follow, he whipped the net from his pouch and twirled it off into the dark.

He gave a tiny grunt of satisfaction. 'Ugh!' He was only seven, but back with the Limpet People he was famous for his hunting skills.

His grandma had taught him. Until that day when she went out alone to hunt a walrus and got killed by its big tusks. Seal still looked for her everywhere. He couldn't believe she was never coming back.

'He's caught it!' cried Coriander.

Something was thrashing about in the net. Seal crowed with triumph. That big insect would make a nice nibble. Seal wasn't fussy about food. Picky eaters didn't live long in Neanderthal times.

They all went running.

'Oh no,' said Smiler. 'It's not the super-louse!'

The luminous bunny stared at them accusingly from inside the net.

'Nice try, Seal,' said Dexter, but even he couldn't help sounding disappointed.

Seal wasn't disappointed. He yelled with delight. This was better than insect! Besides, he'd never trapped a creature that glowed in the dark before. That was useful. A light to make flints by plus your dinner, all in one handy package. He might keep it alive. No, he couldn't. His tummy was rumbling too much.

He held his squirming prey up by the ears. He'd left his best throat-cutting flint behind in Neanderthal times. He was just wondering whether to break the bunny's neck or whop its brains out against the walls, when Smiler and Coriander both shouted, 'No!'

Seal looked up. Did they want to share it? He bared his teeth like a dog. He made growling noises: '*Rurrr!*' They meant, 'Back off! There's hardly enough for me here!'

'Let it go!' said Smiler. He pointed to the bunny. His arms made wide sweeping movements that he hoped meant, 'Give it its freedom!' He did a few bunny hops down the corridor, just to make this extra clear.

Shrill chittering sounds came out of Seal's mouth, like an angry squirrel. They meant, 'Set it free? Have you gone *completely* mad?'

Seal was so busy being surprised that he loosened his grip, just a little. The bunny wriggled free. It leapt to the floor and shot off down the tunnel. Seal went for his net . . .

'No!' shouted Smiler, Coriander and Dexter, all at the same time. Seal stopped in mid-throw. He'd got the message.

It didn't stop him being mad, though. As

his next meal hopped off into the distance, Seal did a stomping dance of rage. He stabbed at them with forked fingers as if he were casting an evil spell. His screams of protest bounced off the metal walls. In Neanderthal times, losing your dinner was a very big deal. You never knew when, or if, you would eat again.

'What do you think he's saying?' asked Coriander. She could speak some Mandarin but she'd never been to after-school classes in Cave Man.

'Dunno,' said Smiler, 'but I bet it's really rude.'

Coriander shrugged. 'Let's get moving. We've got a superlouse to catch.'

'We'll *never* find it!' said Smiler. 'We might as well give up! This fort is like a maze.'

Dexter looked tight-lipped. 'I don't think *finding* it will be the problem.'

'What do you mean?' asked Smiler.

Coriander's voice, smart and cool at the same time, came out of the shadows. 'He means, it needs human heads to survive. He means, the problem will be what to do when it finds *us*.'

'So we're the bait?' Smiler suddenly realized, with a shiver.

'Of course,' said Dexter. 'But what else can we do? Like you said, we could search this place for weeks and never find it. And it mustn't get to the mainland –'

Smiler's frizzy clown wig had gone lopsided on his head. 'This thing is useless!' he fumed. 'That superlouse could easily slide under it.' He sent the wig spinning off into the darkness.

'So what *do* we do when this superlouse finds us?' asked Coriander.

'*Hummm*,' said Dexter. 'Tricky one, that. Just hope Seal gets it, I suppose, before it makes a home on one of our heads.'

They walked on. The tension was terrible. Smiler felt like a sitting target. His eyes were everywhere. The hairs on the back of his neck were wriggling like worms. As they passed his bedroom he suddenly felt an urgent need for something.

'Hang on a mo.'

He nipped in and got his joke book. He thought he'd grown out of it. But these were desperate times. Just stroking its battered blue cover made him feel braver. He stuffed it into his back pocket.

When he rushed out again, Dexter had made a decision. 'Look,' he told Smiler, 'I think it's time we told your grandad what's going on.'

'He's your *grandad*?' said Coriander. 'I thought you were a member of Laughter Club, like me.'

'You must be joking,' said Smiler. 'There's no way I'd *pay* to come to this place!'

As the little group moved off, they missed a faint green sparkle high up in the roof. The giant head louse was clinging to an electricity wire. It was scuttling along it, tracking them every step of the way.

Someone else was already pushing open Grandad's door. It was Dr Maudlin. She didn't realize it was someone's bedroom. But that didn't bother her. She hardly noticed humans. The hunt for her missing superlouse was the only thing that mattered.

Grandad was still snoring gently. As usual, the metal fort sounded as if someone was banging pots and pans together, but this wild jangling didn't keep him awake. He'd found he could live with it. It even lulled him to sleep at night.

Dr Maudlin listened out for scrabbling sounds. She looked in every metal hidey-hole for that telltale green glow. She didn't bother checking Grandad's head. No superlouse could find a home there. Grandad *always* had a Number One at the hairdresser's.

'*Sssssssss.*'

Dr Maudlin was getting seriously rattled. She hadn't planned to release any superlice just yet. She wanted this one safely back in her lab as soon as possible. Her research wasn't complete. There were too many unanswered questions. How long would it live? Would its sons and daughters be superlice too? And there was another flaw in her plan. She wanted *all* head lice to be wiped out, but she seemed to have bred one that was indestructible.

'Where is it?' she gasped through the mask, forgetting that Grandad was there.

Grandad's blue eyes shot open. The racket the iron fort made couldn't wake him, but Dr Maudlin's wheezy Darth Vader voice did.

He lay very quietly, watching. He felt his

stomach scrunch up. He knew there was a person inside there, but that white suit still gave him the creeps. It seemed as if a mad robot had invaded his bedroom.

Dr Maudlin lumbered around. She opened Grandad's sock drawer and tipped all his socks out. She dumped his rock-and-roll CDs on the floor. No head louse.

This is hopeless, she was thinking.

It's hard to do a proper search inside a safety suit. You're cut off from the world, you can't hear very well and you can't see much through the shaded glass. It's like having sunglasses on all the time.

Dr Maudlin hesitated for a second. Then she started pulling off her great, grim helmet. Grandad held his breath.

A tiny head came wobbling out on a neck that looked as thin as a flower stalk. Her face hadn't seen the sun for years. She had sickly white skin, like a mushroom grown in the dark. Her head was nearly bald, except for a fuzz of red hair, as fine as a baby's.

Grandad peered through the gloom. He'd expected what was inside to be *much* scarier.

Feeling brave now, he switched on his bedside lamp.

'Just *what* do you think you're doing?' asked Grandad, angrily.

Dr Maudlin's eyes, pale as tap water, blinked in the sudden light. Her nose was red and drippy. She had a slight cold. What had sounded like menacing hisses and snorts through the mask were just pathetic little sniffles now.

Grandad did a double-take. 'Don't I know you? Didn't we go to the same school together? Aren't you *Violet Matilda* Maudlin?'

Chapter Fourteen

'What happened to you at school was scandalous,' said Grandad. 'It could never happen nowadays!'

It seemed a lifetime ago. Back in the 1950s when they were both about ten years old. But even to Grandad the memory was still painful, and nothing had happened to him. He was just a little boy who could only stand there, feeling helpless.

'That Nit Nurse humiliated you in front of the whole class!' said Grandad.

'I had beautiful long hair the colour of copper,' sniffed Dr Maudlin, who'd pulled up a chair and was sitting beside Grandad's bed.

Now she was out of the helmet she had a tiny, lisping voice. It trilled like a baby bird.

Her eyes looked watery and red. Was she weeping?

'Perhaps we shouldn't talk about it,' suggested Grandad. 'After all, it was a long, long time ago.'

'I remember it as if it were yesterday!' Dr Maudlin's voice was dithery.

She wiped a trembling drip off her nose. Was it snot? Or was it a teardrop? Grandad felt desperately sorry for her. What she'd suffered all those years ago was obviously still haunting her. And no wonder.

Poor, pathetic old dear, he was thinking, even though Dr Maudlin was the same age as him.

'She said I had nits,' sniffled Dr Maudlin. 'She snipped off my hair with big scissors. Then shaved my head with clippers in front of the whole class. All the children made fun of me. I can still hear their mocking laughter.'

'I didn't laugh,' said Grandad.

He'd been horrified as Violet's lovely chestnut tresses had floated to the floor. He remembered her bald head. How white and bumpy it was. How she'd tried to hide it with her hands, then run, crying, from the classroom. She'd never turned up at school again. He'd often wondered what had happened to her.

'As you can see,' said Violet Matilda, pointing to her moth-eaten scalp, 'my hair never grew properly again. It was the shock.'

Grandad shook his head sadly. He didn't know what to say.

Violet Matilda's pale eyes suddenly flashed with pure hatred. 'If that Nit Nurse were alive today, I'd string her up from the nearest tree. I'd make sure she suffered as much as I did, the evil old witch!'

Well, you can't blame Violet, thought Grandad. It must have been a dreadful experience.

But even he was made a bit uneasy by the cruel glee in Dr Maudlin's voice. And by the fact that she still dreamed of revenge after fifty years.

'So if I couldn't get the Nit Nurse,' Dr Maudlin was telling him, 'the nits were the next best thing. I never recovered from that classroom humiliation. Head lice were the cause of all my misery. I decided they didn't deserve to live. I decided to wipe them off the face of the earth!'

'Oh, right,' said Grandad slowly, wondering if he ought to call for help.

'I married, I had a son, but I never got over it!' raved Dr Maudlin. 'Do you think I wear this blasted suit because I'm paranoid about parasites? No!' She gave a shrill, bitter laugh. 'They could hardly survive on *my* head! I hide inside it so I don't have to face the world. A world that treated me so cruelly!'

Phew, thought Grandad. I think I'm out of my depth here.

'By the way,' Dr Maudlin added in a calmer voice, 'you can relax. It's not in here. I've checked. Trust me, I know their evil little ways. I can even *think* like they do.'

Eh? thought Grandad. What's she on about? What's not in here? Is this woman a total loony?

He'd been a bit left behind by events. He still thought Dr Maudlin was doing research into jellyfish.

Neither of them noticed that Dr Maudlin had left the bedroom door open. Or that two green clown shoes with pink dots had sneaked in. Dexter was lurking outside. Along with Smiler and Coriander, he was eavesdropping.

They'd been about to barge in, but when they heard voices, they shrank back into the shadows. Seal was with them. He wasn't interested in what was going on in Grandad's bedroom. He was sitting cross-legged on the floor. He'd got his limpet spoon out. He was tucking into his four emergency limpets. They were a bit smelly by now, a bit tough and chewy, but Seal still smacked his lips. Eating always made him feel happy.

'What's that awful smell?' said Grandad, wrinkling his nose. 'Like dead crabs!' He looked towards the door. He saw two green, spotty toes peeking in.

'Mr Funny Bones? Is that you?'

Dexter shuffled inside. After what he'd just overheard, he felt almost torn in two. Should he, *could* he, forgive Dr Maudlin for his neglected childhood? Now that he'd finally found out the reason why?

'Mother!' he cried, flapping his soggy palms. 'You should have told me *why* you hated head lice! Then I might have understood!'

Outside in the corridor, Smiler and Coriander hung back. This was a private moment between Dexter and his mother. They didn't want to play gooseberry. On the other hand, it was a louse-free zone in there. They'd heard Dr Maudlin say so.

The superlouse, squashed into a crack in the ceiling, looked down on Smiler, Coriander and Seal. Seal's hair would have made a good home. Like living in a wild, tangled wood. But the head louse happened to be directly above Smiler. It was *his* head it was eyeballing, and it had made its decision: '*That head is mine!*'

It slid halfway out of the crack. It got ready to make a flying leap.

A second before it was about to jump, Smiler said, 'I'm not staying out here!'

He and Coriander crowded in behind Dexter.

The superlouse squeezed itself back into its hiding place.

'It's still out there somewhere,' Smiler whispered to Coriander. 'Make sure you shut that door!'

'Where's Seal?'

'Oh no, I nearly forgot.'

Smiler dashed outside and yanked Seal in. The head louse was taken by surprise. It nearly jumped, but its head was long gone. Never mind. It settled back down to wait. Smiler was a marked man. There was no way he could escape.

Grandad hadn't noticed the little group by the door. He was too busy staring from Dexter to Dr Maudlin and back again: 'Did you just call her *Mother*?'

So Smiler and Coriander shoved Seal behind them. They didn't want Grandad to see him just yet. Grandad already had enough shocks coming.

'That having all her hair shaved off, in front of the whole class – it must have been awful!' Smiler whispered to Coriander.

But Coriander didn't feel so sympathetic. 'She should have got over it by now!' she said crisply. 'Look what trouble she's caused.'

Smiler took a long look at the person inside the safety suit. He was amazed. Had that tiny, bird-like, drippy thing really been the scary Giant Maggot? Even if you didn't know, you could have guessed that she and Dexter were related. They both had sharp, quivering noses. And they were both very *soggy* people.

Everyone looked upset – Grandad, Dr Maudlin, Dexter. That made Smiler upset too. 'Tell them a joke!' his heart told him before his mind could stop it.

His voice roared into the silence, 'What's green and hairy and goes up and down?'

Every face turned to stare at him. Oh no! thought Smiler, cringing. They're not laughing! I've messed up again! Maybe he should have looked in his joke book for something funnier.

But he had no time to get embarrassed because, just at that moment, Seal stumbled out from behind them, yawning and rubbing his eyes. In one astonished look, Grandad took in his monkey-shaped body, his big hooter and strange, flat-topped head.

'Who is this child?' he demanded.

'He's one of the peaceful Limpet People,' said Coriander, as if it was obvious. 'They used to live where this fort is now.'

Seal waddled up to Grandad. He peered

at him through shaggy hair. He gave him a big sniff. Nothing threatening there. Then he pitched forward, face down, on to Grandad's bed. Like a baby, he was instantly fast asleep.

Grandad struggled out from under Seal's sleeping body. Smiler couldn't help wincing. As well as his T-shirt, Grandad had skimpy shorts on that said 'Wild Thing' across the front.

I know Grandad's cool, thought Smiler, but that's going a bit far. Especially with his veiny legs.

Slowly, locking eyes with each one in turn, Grandad gave them his teacher's glare. He hadn't lost the knack. It made them all, even Dr Maudlin, feel like naughty schoolkids.

'Now that you've invaded my bedroom,' he told them, sternly, 'hadn't you better tell me what on *earth's* going on?'

Coriander and Smiler did all the talking. Dexter and Dr Maudlin were strangely silent. They kept sneaking uneasy glances at each other. Had anything changed between mother and son? It was too soon to say.

Seal twitched in his sleep like a dog. He was dreaming about home. About diving in deep, seaweedy pools with his mother, and climbing up cliffs with his sister to get gulls' eggs.

It was Coriander who did most of the explaining. Crazy things were happening here on the fort. There were so many mysteries, so many answers she didn't know. She wasn't used to things being so unpredictable but, on the plus side, she'd never felt so alive in her whole life.

'So this superlouse has *got* to be caught,' she told Grandad. 'And none of the others must be released. They'll wipe out an entire species.'

'And what about us kids?' insisted Smiler. '*I* decide what happens on *my* head. Not some superlouse. I'm not a violent person. I don't want World War III going on up there!'

While they talked, strange things were also occurring outside, in the estuary. It was low tide, but the wind was rising. The night sky was completely clear except for dense black clouds gathering right over the fort. Only Seal felt it. He shivered in his sleep, as if he felt the storm coming.

'And what about when this superlouse

starts flashing on and off?' demanded Smiler. He'd become a bit obsessed about that.

'Why would it flash on and off?' asked Grandad.

'You don't want to know,' said Smiler.

He started scratching again. He just couldn't help it.

'Is that it?' asked Grandad, when they finally stopped speaking.

Grandad didn't know who to be angry with first. With himself, for only thinking about Laughter Club and not knowing what was going on right under his nose. With Smiler, for not telling him sooner. With Dexter, for lying about his clown qualifications. Or with Dr Maudlin, for using his fort for such dodgy research.

Then Seal, still asleep, kicked out. One of his sand-dune grass shoes slipped off.

'He's got webbed feet!' said Grandad.

'I already *explained* about that,' said Coriander, briskly, as if Grandad should get a grip. 'And about his occipital bun.'

'She's been to after-school Archaeology classes,' said Smiler.

'Advanced,' added Coriander.

Did she explain? thought Grandad. His head was spinning. It was all too much to take in, but it began to dawn on him that, just *maybe*, he was looking at a child who had walked the earth thousands of years ago.

Grandad forgot about superlice. '*Is it possible?*' he whispered, gazing at Seal. He seemed thunderstruck. He could hardly get the words out.

'Don't worry. *We* felt like you,' said Smiler, nodding towards Coriander, 'when *we* first realized.'

'But how did he get here?' asked Grandad, his voice stronger.

'Ask her,' said Dexter.

They turned, and stared accusingly at Dr Maudlin.

'We're waiting, Mother,' warned Dexter, tapping his spotty clown shoe.

Chapter Fifteen

Outside, the black clouds seemed close to bursting. Every few seconds, they were eerily lit up from inside by electric-blue flashes. Soon, the lightning would split the clouds. It would come sizzling out of the sky and strike the fort.

The metal-eating slime mould wasn't wasting any time. It had multiplied millions of times and glowed even brighter green. Now it looked like a tide of toxic sludge. It had an enormous appetite and it had munched its way through the basement floor. It was starting to flow down the iron legs of the fort, chomping away as it went.

Back in Grandad's bedroom, everyone was still waiting for Dr Maudlin to speak.

She blinked her strange, insipid eyes. They

had about as much colour as icicles. She looked irritated, as if talking about anything but head lice was a waste of her time.

'It was the night of the last big storm,' she twittered. Her voice was tiny, now she was out of the helmet. You had to listen very hard to hear it.

'I found him wandering about on the fort. Who knows how he ended up here?' She shrugged, as if it didn't interest her. 'Perhaps some kind of massive build-up of electrical energy pulled him through time –'

'I said that!' blurted out Smiler. 'Remember, Coriander? I said this fort was like a giant magnet.'

Privately, Coriander had to admit, Smiler's sometimes silly. But he's smart too. Why had her parents told her those two things could never go together?

Dr Maudlin ignored Smiler. 'The *really* fascinating thing,' she continued, 'is that this Neanderthal boy's hair contained some very *exciting* head lice. I'd never seen anything like them! I was able to use them as the basis of all my experiments –'

Crack! A jagged bolt of blue fire hit the fort.

It fizzed between the lightning conductors. Seal's eyes shot open. He looked at them all in bewilderment. He saw Dr Maudlin. She didn't have a White Monster head any more, but he still seemed scared of her.

It was Dexter he scurried to for protection. Dexter's lip trembled with emotion because Seal had chosen him.

'It's all right,' he said, as the scared Stone Age boy huddled in next to him. 'I won't let anyone hurt you.'

'Fall over, Mr Funny Bones!' roared Smiler, like a circus ringmaster. 'Make him laugh!'

Coriander gave him a sideways look.

'*Whoops!*' said Smiler, giving his forehead a good smack. 'You're right, Coriander. This is no time for slapstick!' He'd only wanted to see a smile on Seal's face.

Crack! This time everyone was startled.

'That sounds like a humdinger of a storm,' said Grandad.

Just like the last time, the iron fort was right at the centre of it. It crackled with energy and power. The unearthly blue glow spread through the porthole into Grandad's bedroom. When it washed over Seal something strange happened. He lifted his head like a dog and sniffed the air. Then, even without Mr Funny Bones falling over, a smile lit up his face. What could he smell? Was it *home*?

Seal got up and peered through a porthole. He made loud, excited cries, shrill as seagulls. What had he seen in the night sky? Mr Funny Bones looked out too, but all he could see were stars.

Those stars meant something to Seal, though. His seagull cries got shriller. He kicked off his other shoe. He toddled, as fast as his webbed feet would let him, out of the door. He didn't have far to go. The landing stage was very close.

'Seal!' shouted Dexter. 'Come back. There's a big storm out there!'

He dashed after him. Coriander and Smiler followed. The superlouse, flattened into its hidey-hole, saw its own personal head go rushing by. A deadly green disc dropped out of the ceiling. It inflated to full size on the way down, its claws out, ready to cling . . .

'Hang on!' said Smiler. 'I've just got to tie this shoelace.' He bent down.

The superlouse missed him by millimetres. Smiler didn't even see it. It landed with a soft, springy *ping!* on the metal floor and scuttled off into the dark. Smiler had got away . . . but not for long. The superlouse would come looking for him again. It would seek out his head like a guided missile. It would never, *ever* give up.

Smiler and Coriander skidded out on to the landing stage.

'Where's Seal?' said Smiler.

'I don't know!' replied Dexter, leaning over the rail and looking down.

'What's happened to the storm?' asked Coriander, staring around her.

The three of them gazed in every direction. The shrieking wind had stopped. It was dead calm. There was a strange hush over the estuary. Then a huge silver moon came gliding over the horizon, flooding the mud flats with a magical silver glow.

'The stars have changed!' said Coriander, not bothering to add that she'd once done an after-school Astronomy class.

'You're right,' said Mr Funny Bones, who was a bit of an astronomy buff himself.

'What kind of sky is *that*?'

Only Seal had recognized it. He knew the patterns of the stars by heart – the Limpet People used them to navigate. Smiler, Coriander and Dexter hadn't caught on yet, but they were staring at a Stone Age sky – before the space age had filled it with junk. All the modern-day satellites, that usually sparkle in the dark, were missing.

Smiler shivered. The air was electric. They could all feel it, tingling through to their bones. For a few minutes, it felt like time had stopped. The fort wasn't making its mad metal music any more. The thunder and lightning were taking a rest.

Something momentous was happening. Smiler knew it. Coriander did too. Hairs were lifting on the back of her neck.

'Seal must have gone down the ladder,' whispered Coriander. You felt you had to whisper in the awesome silence.

Dexter went down first. He noticed that something spongy and luminous green had almost hidden the great iron stilts that supported the fort.

He thought, That's strange seaweed.

He'd check it out later. Not now. He was too worried about Seal.

'Seal!'

Seal was standing on the slab of rock by the fossil footprints.

Somehow, he knew instinctively what to do to get home. Carefully, he placed his feet inside the last two footprints. Of course, they were a perfect fit. Smiler was right. They were Seal's own footprints. He'd been standing on this very spot about 30,000 years ago when the powerful magnetic pull of the iron fort had dragged him through time.

'Seal!' Dexter clattered over the rock in his big clown's shoes. He reached out to touch Seal. But his hand went through empty air. Seal had vanished.

Coriander and Smiler were only seconds behind.

'Where's he gone?' said Coriander, looking around.

Smiler gazed into the dark, mysterious eel pool and asked, 'Has he gone diving in there for his dinner?'

'No.' As he spoke, Dexter was unlacing his long clown's shoes. He pulled them off.

Inside, his bare feet were dainty and
surprisingly small.

'I think he's gone back.'

'*What?*' said Smiler.

'He just did this.' Dexter stepped into the
fossil footprints. He jiggled his feet about to
make them fit. For an instant, his body was
still there. Then it grew transparent and
watery. It rippled like the surface of a pond
and in a second it was gone.

Coriander and Smiler stared at the place
where Dexter had just been. They were too
shocked to speak.

The iron fort loomed above them. *Clink,*
clink. Its music was starting up. Very softly,
the thunder growled. The eel pool was
suddenly ruffled with tiny waves. The wind
was rising again.

Coriander recovered first. She took her
shoes off.

'Quick, stand in Seal's footprints. They're
the way through. Like a gateway! But it's
closing up.'

'What are you talking about?' gabbled
Smiler. 'What are you doing?' He looked
around wildly. 'Where's Grandad?'

'I've got to *see*,' said Coriander. She was trembling, but she sounded excited. 'I've got to see where Seal comes from.'

'You're crazy!' said Smiler.

'The storm's starting again!' shouted Coriander, as the wind whipped her hair. 'The fort'll pull us back here again, if we stay in the footprints. Come on! This is our only chance.'

How does she *know* all that? thought Smiler. Had she done an after-school class in Time Travel? Or was she just guessing?

'You're supposed to be the sensible one!' he shouted at her, angrily. 'It's *me* that says silly things!'

Why did she trust the iron fort to protect them? Especially when she'd said before that it never obeyed the rules!

Smiler clutched his joke book. It didn't make him feel any better. His mind was still a mad, panicking whirl. He grabbed her arm. 'We could end up anywhere. What if we're stuck there?'

Coriander seemed strangely calm now. 'I can't help it. I've got to *see*. Or I'll always regret it. You coming or what?'

In a dream, Smiler kicked off his trainers. He peeled off his socks and stuffed them neatly inside. She wasn't daring him. She wasn't calling him pathetic. She was speaking to him like a serious person who could make big, important decisions. Not like some silly little pest she didn't want tagging along. And that was probably why he went.

At the same time as she did, Smiler stepped on to the stone footprints.

As they vanished, a savage crack of lightning hit the fort. The storm started up again just as Grandad rushed out on to the landing stage. He'd wasted precious minutes trying to find his jeans and shoes and socks.

'Smiler! Coriander!' he yelled into the howling wind. Metal clanged all around him. Why was the platform wobbling? He clung on to the rail.

'Is this fort rocking on its legs? I must be imagining it. I'm going mad!' He looked around desperately. 'Smiler, Coriander, Dexter! Where are you?'

He almost didn't make it down the ladder. It was shaking and bucking, as if it was trying to throw him off. Surely, thought Grandad, as he clung on grimly, the storm can't be causing this? The iron fort had stood firm through two World Wars!

At last, he was safe on solid rock. But straight away his heart clenched like a fist. Lined up in front of him he saw three pairs of shoes. Smiler's, Coriander's and two green clown shoes with pink spots.

'Oh no!' Grandad hurled himself down to the eel pool. Frantically, he stared into its green, seaweedy depths. 'They haven't drowned, have they?'

He could hardly see in the darkness, but a sudden flash of lightning helped him out. Thank heavens, he thought.

There were no bodies down there. Only writhing eels and sea anemones waving their tentacles at him.

He didn't twig about the footprints. Even if he had, he couldn't have taken the same route as the others through time. His feet were too big. They wouldn't fit inside Seal's footprints.

He was shouting 'Smiler!' again when a wheezy voice gasped into his ear. 'I'm going to save my head louse.'

Grandad spun round. It was Dr Maudlin. She was hidden inside her white helmet again. Grandad stared through the black glass of the mask, but he couldn't see her eyes.

'What are you *talking* about?' he shrieked at her. 'My grandson's missing. So is Coriander. Your *own son* is missing! What's wrong with you? Forget about your stupid superlouse!'

For a second, Dr Maudlin seemed to hesitate. Then she grunted something and started climbing back up the shaky ladder.

Grandad forgot about her.

'Maybe they've started walking to the mainland.' He stepped off the rock. *Gloop!* His foot sank straight into the mud. He stared out over the estuary.

He could see lights moving across the dark mud flats. Were they torches? He could hear wild cries and shrieks carried on the storm. What was going on out there? It sounded like something terrible. Were Smiler and Coriander caught up in the middle of it?

Chapter Sixteen

Afterwards, Smiler could never remember exactly how he and Coriander seemed to step through a door into the Stone Age. It was – so *easy*. As if circumstances were just right – the iron fort, the storm, the fossil footprints – to mix up Neanderthal times and the twenty-first century for a few amazing moments.

The world around them dissolved into ripples. When it reassembled itself it was still a bright moonlit night, but there was no fort above them. And no storm. They were standing on a wild, rocky shore. Great heaps of rotting seaweed, on a wide, white beach, stretched away into the distance.

Smiler rubbed his eyes. 'Where are we?' he said, in a stunned voice. 'Where are Seal and Dexter?'

He should have been petrified. Why aren't I wetting my pants? he wondered. But his brain didn't seem to be working properly. Parts of it seemed to have just closed down, as if it couldn't cope with the overload.

'We're in the same place we started out,' said a voice in his ear. He whirled round. Coriander was just behind him. 'Only this is like it was thousands of years ago when the Limpet People lived here. Brilliant, isn't it?'

Smiler wasn't so sure. 'What have you done?' he groaned at himself, *thwacking* his forehead a few times. 'This is the biggest mess I've ever got myself into!' he told Coriander.

Suddenly Coriander felt a strong pulling sensation, as if she was wearing braces and someone behind her was stretching them.

'I don't think we're going to be here long,' she said.

Smiler staggered backwards. He'd felt it too.

'It's the iron fort!' Relief swept over him. 'It's keeping hold of us!' At least they weren't abandoned here. They'd be *boinged* back soon, into the twenty-first century, as if they were on elastic.

He dared to wander a few steps. His

numbed brain kept telling him, 'Guess what? You're in Neanderthal times!'

'Don't go far,' warned Coriander. 'If we move from this spot, the fort might not be able to reach us.'

It was true. The further away Smiler moved, the less he felt the fort's influence. He rushed back to stand in front of Coriander. Straight away, the tugging on his spine started up again.

'But where are Seal and Dexter?' he said, looking around frantically. 'They should be here! Wait a second, there are some people. Look, coming out from those sand dunes. Seal's with them! Hey, Seal!'

'*Shhh!*' said Coriander. 'Don't scare 'em.'

They were some of the shy, peaceful Limpet People. Seal's mother and sister, an uncle, some cousins. All with big hooters like him and shaggy hair and webbed feet. They all shared the same fishy stink. They clustered round Seal, crying out welcomes, their shrill, piping voices like sea birds.

They sniffed at him. They put hands out to touch him, patting and stroking him, as if they couldn't believe he wasn't a ghost.

'*Awwwww!*' said Smiler.

He felt a bright glow warming his whole body. He was glad now he'd come. He wouldn't have missed this happy meeting for anything.

'Isn't that great?' he said to Coriander. 'I bet that's his family! For heaven's sake,' he said, embarrassed, 'I'm getting all soppy now! I'm going to be crying in a minute. How silly is that?'

'It's not silly at all,' said Coriander, wiping away a tear.

'They'll see us if we don't watch out,' said Smiler.

'Don't move,' Coriander warned him again.

'You must be joking,' said Smiler. 'I'm staying right here.' He craned his neck round. 'Where's Dexter? He'd better hurry up.'

The Neanderthal world was already going fuzzy at the edges.

Suddenly his body jerked backwards as if someone was yanking an invisible rope round his waist. 'There isn't much time!' shouted Smiler.

Even if he'd wanted to stay, it was no use fighting against the power of the iron fort.

Someone came racing out of the sand dunes. There was no mistaking those baggy clown trousers, that frizzy orange hair. It was Dexter. He didn't even see Smiler and Coriander. He was waving his arms to warn the Limpet People. 'Run! Run for your lives! You're being attacked!'

A warlike whoop burst out of the darkness.

Seal's mum stared around, alarmed. She looked very young and scared. She clutched Seal to her.

'What's going on!' said Smiler, trying to see while the beach got more and more blurry.

'Dexter!' yelled Coriander, as the tugging of the iron fort became urgent. 'Come back to us! Or you'll be too late!'

Dexter turned round. He'd heard her. But there was a dreadful struggle going on inside him.

'Quick!' shouted Smiler. 'There's no time left!'

The world around Smiler and Coriander

was rippling and breaking up. It was like looking through dark, wavy glass. Sounds were getting fainter. But they both heard Dexter's amazing answer: 'I can't leave Seal! I'm staying here!'

They saw Dexter racing towards the little family group. They were huddled together like terrified rabbits.

Suddenly the night sky was filled with savage howls.

'They're here! Hide! Hide!' shrieked Dexter.

He showed them how. He dived into a great heap of rotting seaweed. The smell nearly made him choke. He started pulling it over his head. Hope flashed across Seal's mum's face. She looked at Dexter as if he was a hero.

Seal buried himself in seaweed too. The rest of the family copied him. Soon they were all hidden. They were only just in time.

Dark shapes came shambling out of the sand dunes. It was the rest of the Limpet People. They were frantic to reach the sea to swim away. But with their clumsy webbed feet they didn't stand a chance. Another tribe, much faster and fiercer, came swarming after them. They were tall and slim, streaked with blue war paint. They carried fiery torches. And clubs and spears.

'Cro-Magnons!' said Coriander in a voice filled with horror. 'Modern humans!'

The moon was swallowed up by clouds. The Cro-Magnons chased the Limpet People into the darkness. Red torches bobbed about. There were cries and screams . . .

These were Smiler and Coriander's last few seconds in the Stone Age. They felt themselves being scooped up, as if by a giant invisible hand.

'Dexter! Seal! We're going!'

But they were already too far away for anyone in the Stone Age to hear.

Chapter Seventeen

Dr Maudlin was deep in the maze-like tunnels at the heart of the iron fort. The dim yellow lights kept flickering on and off. Every now and again the metal floor gave a lurch. It was like being on a ship at sea.

But Dr Maudlin hardly noticed that the whole fort was shaking. You don't feel anything much, shut up inside a safety suit. Besides, her mind was fixed on only one thing – getting her superlouse back.

The green glowing rabbit felt the vibrations.

'Danger!' its bunny brain told it. 'Get out of here!'

It scooted past Dr Maudlin. She didn't see it.

Back in the lab, the other superlice sensed

something was happening. They rattled their claws on the glass of their tanks. They hurled their bodies against the sides, trying to smash their way out.

Rurrr! Rurrr! As she stomped along, Dr Maudlin's breath came gasping through the helmet. What was that? She swivelled that grim head. Her vision inside there wasn't too good, but she'd spotted something glowing between the iron plates. She stopped. Was it the superlouse?

Words came snorting out of the mask. 'Come here, my precious. Come to Mummy.'

Down by the eel pool, Grandad was looking around him in shock and horror. Something had happened to the great iron legs. For a start, they glowed green in the dark, but, much more serious than that, they were buckling. They couldn't support the fort's weight any more and bits of it were falling off.

Instead of clanging metal music, Grandad heard the crunch and groan of iron plates ripping apart. *Clang!* He winced as a gun turret came crashing down. Grandad didn't know it, but the Grey Guardian, which had survived submarine and fighter-plane attacks, was finally being destroyed by slimy Stone Age microbes.

Grandad should have legged it, sharpish. But he was too worried about the others to save himself.

The storm was fading away. Then – *crack!* – just before it died, a jagged flash of lightning hit the fort dead centre. Once again, the whole thing seemed to burn like a blue fireball. But the blaze was weaker. It was the last of its strength.

'Grandad! Over here!'

Grandad's face lit up with happiness. 'Smiler! Coriander! You're safe!'

Smiler staggered up from the rock where he'd been sprawling. He shook himself like a dog. '*Phew!* I feel dizzy. What was all that about?'

'I think we nearly didn't make it back,' gasped Coriander.

They'd been sucked through a swirling time tunnel, speeding as fast as a tube train. He remembered lights, rings of colour whizzing round him, but then they'd slowed down. The tunnel walls started squeezing in, like a great throat closing.

Smiler had thought, We're trapped! Then, with one mighty heave, they were hauled back into the twenty-first century.

'I don't think anyone else will get through,' said Coriander, her face solemn.

'If they're still alive,' mumbled Smiler. He couldn't bear to think about it. 'What if those Cro-Magnons came back and found them?'

'They didn't find them,' said Coriander.

'How do you know? You don't know everything!'

'What are you talking about?' interrupted Grandad. 'Where were you? I was worried sick. And where are the others?'

'They're safe,' Coriander told Grandad.

'How do you know that? Tell me!' shouted Smiler, clenching his fists in frustration.

'Well –' began Coriander.

A deafening, booming noise came from above their heads. It echoed for miles across the dark estuary. BOOM! There it went again. The iron fort was breaking up.

'Hey!' said Smiler. 'These legs are all wonky!'

'We've got to get out from under here!'

yelled Grandad. 'The fort's not going to last much longer.'

Ping, ping, ping. Metal bolts came flying out like machine-gun bullets.

'Get to a safe distance!' shrieked Grandad, shooing them away.

'Stay on the water pipe!' Smiler shouted to Coriander above the terrible din of the dying fort. 'Watch out for the mud!'

Why wasn't Grandad coming with them? Why was he still dithering at the bottom of the iron ladder?

'Hurry up, Grandad!' screamed Smiler. He ran back along the pipe to grab his arm.

'Dr Maudlin's still in there,' said Grandad. 'I've got to warn her.'

'You can't climb that!' roared Smiler. 'It's half hanging off. And what's that green slimy stuff? It's everywhere!'

Grandad put his foot on the bottom rung.

'Look out!' yelled Smiler, as the sound of metal being mangled came from right overhead. They started running back along the pipe. The ladder and the landing stage came crashing down in a twisted heap just where they'd been standing.

'No one can get in there now,' sighed Smiler. 'She's on her own.'

By now, even Dr Maudlin, inside her safety suit, knew that something was up. All around her, metal corridors were collapsing in on themselves. She knew she had to get out. But she wasn't going to leave without her superlouse.

'Come out,' she coaxed in her gurgling voice.

A strange thing had happened. Dr Maudlin had spent most of her life hating head lice, trying to wipe them off the face of the earth. But now she'd found a head louse she couldn't bear to kill. It was her own creation. She was proud of it.

The superlouse slid out of its hidey-hole. Did it feel any affection for Dr Maudlin? Or was it just looking for a human head to feed on? The floor was swaying so much, Dr Maudlin found it hard to stand. *Crash!* Another corridor caved in. Her last escape route was cut off. But she didn't care.

'*Awww!*' she said, as the superlouse glowed brilliant green and inflated itself to its full size. 'Who's a good boy then? Come to Mummy.'

For the first time in years and years, all the hatred was washed from her mind and she felt something very like love.

At that very moment, a massive iron plate fell from the tunnel roof. Violet Matilda Maudlin and her superlouse were squashed flat. Neither of them felt a thing.

Dr Maudlin never knew that none of her other head lice had survived either. The lab had been one of the first places to go. It was crushed like an empty Coke can. Even superlice never stood a chance.

A safe distance away, Smiler, Coriander and Grandad stood crowded together on the water pipe.

It was like watching the *Titanic* go down from the lifeboats. The Grey Guardian didn't give up without a fight, but in the end, with one last great groan, the legs snapped in two and what was left of the fort came crashing down. Seal's fossil footprints were smashed into smithereens.

Smiler couldn't believe it. The iron fort was gone. A few minutes ago it had been mightier than a medieval castle. A strange, scary, magical place. Now it was just a big scrapyard.

Coriander sounded as upset as he was.

'I was beginning to like being there,' she said.

Grandad didn't comment. He thought he hadn't heard right. 'You're still in shock,' he told himself. 'She can't have said that. Laughter Club's been a total disaster!'

Grandad stared back at the wreckage. He shook his head sadly, 'Nothing could have lived through that,' he said. 'It's the end of Dr Maudlin.'

'And it's the end of that cool, fluorescent rabbit,' Smiler mourned. He felt really gutted about that.

'For heaven's sake, Smiler,' said Grandad angrily. 'What's a rabbit matter? We're talking about a human life here!'

This is awful, thought Smiler. Everyone's upset! Grandad's snapping my head off! What have I said?

Was it time to tell a joke? He fumbled in his pocket for his joke book. What about that cuckoo-clock one? That might cheer Grandad up.

But his pocket was empty.

'Oh no,' roared Smiler, smacking his hand

off his forehead. 'Am I an idiot or what? Do you know what I've done? I've gone and left my joke book behind in Neanderthal times!'

'That's tragic,' said Coriander, carefully keeping her face straight.

There were streaks of pink in the eastern sky. A chill wind was coming over the mud flats. 'It's dawn,' said Grandad, shivering. 'We'd better move from here. The sea's coming in.'

Beep, beep, beep, beep.

'What's that?' said Grandad.

'It's my mobile,' said Coriander, digging in her pocket. 'I forgot I had it with me.'

'Can I borrow it?' asked Grandad. 'I need to call the emergency services.'

'Hang on,' said Coriander. 'I've got a text message.' She stared at the tiny screen.

'What's it say?' asked Smiler.

He suddenly had the wild idea that Dexter was text messaging them from the Stone Age to say that he and Seal were still alive.

'It's from my parents,' said Coriander.

'Oh,' said Smiler, badly disappointed. 'What do *they* want?'

Coriander showed him the screen. It said, '*bsnss gn bst. bth lst jbs.*'

'So? What's that mean?' asked Smiler.

'It means,' replied Coriander, 'that the business they worked for has gone bust. They're not important executives any more.'

'And they want you to worry about little things like *that*!' said Smiler. 'After what's happened to us tonight? They must be *joking*!'

Chapter Eighteen

Smiler and Coriander were sitting in the sand dunes at the edge of the estuary. Three months had passed since the iron fort collapsed.

'Explain it to me again,' said Smiler. 'How do you *know* that Dexter and Seal and his family got away?'

Coriander raised her eyebrows. 'I've told you *hundreds* of times before.'

'I know. But I just like hearing about it.'

It gave him a big buzz of happiness to know that Dexter and his little band of Limpet People had escaped the terrible Cro-Magnon attack.

Coriander sighed. 'It's because of Dexter's red hair, right? Scientists have proved that we modern humans inherited our red hair from Neanderthals. You know, it got passed on through their genes. But they couldn't work out *how*. Because Neanderthals weren't supposed to have mated with Cro-Magnons. They were supposed to have just died out.'

Smiler squirmed uneasily. This was the bit he didn't like. All that talk about mating. He'd had quite enough of that with the giant superlouse.

'So you're saying Dexter must have survived. And got a Limpet People girlfriend and had kids?'

Coriander shrugged, 'Yep. I bet it was Seal's mum. She was about the same age as him. And did you see those *adoring* looks she was giving him?'

Smiler felt extra happy with that idea. Dexter and Seal had been really close. He just loved thinking that Dexter had ended up as Seal's dad. What good laughs they would have together! And, after a while, you probably didn't even notice the smell . . .

'I mean, I'm not *certain* it happened like that,' admitted Coriander.

'Yeah, but you're bound to be right!' said Smiler, confidently.

'Probably,' agreed Coriander. 'And all those scientists who say Neanderthals didn't mate with modern humans are wrong! They mated with a human from the twenty-first century. So Dr Maudlin actually inherited her red hair from her own son.'

Smiler frowned. 'This is making my brain ache,' he said.

He sidetracked to another thing that puzzled him.

'So if Dexter and Seal's mum had kids, how come some of us haven't got webbed feet?'

Coriander didn't seem at all stumped by that question. 'Some things get passed on, like red-hair genes. And some things don't – like webbed-feet genes. It's the lottery of evolution.'

'Oh . . . right,' said Smiler, slowly. 'Let's talk about something else! What about that green glowing rabbit? Give me some reasons why he could have survived.'

'I can't,' said Coriander, sadly. 'That would be silly.'

They both stared out at the wreck of the iron fort. Sand had drifted over it. You couldn't even tell it had been there. But Coriander was right. Nothing could survive that kind of damage. Dr Maudlin hadn't. Even the superlice had been crushed. A bunny would stand no chance at all.

'Do you think that cloud up there looks like a castle?' Coriander asked, suddenly.

The first time she'd asked him this, Smiler had almost passed out with shock. Coriander cloud watching! It seemed about as likely as his head teacher, Mr Braithwaite, playing with ducks in the bath.

But he was used to it now. After all, they'd both had a lot of time for cloud watching lately. Ever since Grandad and Coriander's parents had become business partners. They'd opened the Laugh Yourself Slim Club. To Smiler's surprise, it was a wild success. Now they were opening a whole chain of them, all across the country. They even planned to expand to America.

'I've given up most of my after-school classes,' Coriander told Smiler. 'Like Extra Algebra. Mum's too busy to take me.'

'I bet you're really sad about that!' grinned Smiler.

'Devastated,' said Coriander, grinning back.

Smiler had got used to her grinning too. She hadn't done a big belly laugh yet. But you can't expect miracles.

And, amazingly, Smiler felt quite relaxed about that. He didn't feel frantic to make people laugh any more. Not all the time anyway.

'Why does an elephant paint the bottom of its feet yellow?'

Coriander groaned. She pretended she hadn't heard.

'Have you heard from your grandad lately?'

'Oh, he's having a great time.'

It was a perfect partnership. Coriander's mum and dad did the boring bits. They managed the business while Grandad did the publicity. He was in California at the moment, telling people about his Laugh Yourself Slim philosophy.

'Why go on a diet?' Grandad asked them. 'Why get sweaty down at the gym? Watch a funny video instead. Crack a few jokes. Laughter is the new way to lose weight! You don't even have to move off your chair.'

His talks went down a storm. So did the book he'd just written. He became a slimming guru! He was invited on breakfast TV shows.

'If you belly laugh for five minutes you use up one *hundred* calories,' Grandad told viewers. 'Even a little titter uses up ten!' It was just what everyone wanted to hear.

'He's going out to wild parties every night! He's meeting famous film stars!' Smiler told Coriander. 'My dad says he should be ashamed of himself, at his age, carrying on like that.'

'Does it work?' asked Coriander, doubtfully. 'You know, laughing yourself slim.'

'Dunno,' said Smiler, 'but who cares? Grandad says everyone leaves his Laugh Yourself Slim Clubs feeling so good, they stop worrying about not looking like supermodels.'

Smiler lay back on the warm white sand. For a few seconds, he watched the clouds race by. Then he said, 'I miss Seal and Dexter. But I suppose Seal had to go back, didn't he?'

He just wouldn't have fitted in. How could you have a Neanderthal kid in a twenty-first-century school?

On the other hand, thought Smiler,

thinking of some of his mates, he might not have stood out that much.

'I wish Dexter could come back, though,' said Smiler. 'He never knew that ordinary head lice didn't get wiped out.' Smiler stopped to give his head a good scratch. 'I wish I could tell him that.'

'But we'd have to tell him his mum died,' Coriander pointed out. 'That she didn't change. Right to the end, she was more worried about her superlouse than she was about him!'

'He's better off where he is,' Smiler suddenly decided. 'Bet Seal's family love him. Bet he's a hero back in the Stone Age. And the funniest guy on the planet.'

'Anyway, that reminds me,' said Coriander. 'I've got a present for you. I picked it up on the mud flats.'

She held out something small and white. At first, Smiler thought it was Seal's flute: 'Oh, brilliant!' But when he saw it was a limpet spoon, he was even more thrilled. He took it, reverently.

'I'll keep it always! Think I should use it,' he fretted, 'to eat ice cream, for instance?

Because I'm not a big fan of limpets. Or should I keep it safe in my bedroom drawer? What would Seal want me to do?'

'*Shhh!*' Coriander put a finger to her lips. 'Look there!'

Very, very carefully, Smiler turned his head. Out of the corner of his eye, he saw a green glow in a shadowy scoop between the dunes.

He thought, 'Oh no, a superlouse survived!'

He started panicking. He jammed his baseball cap right down on his head. 'Is all my hair hidden?'

But then he saw two long floppy ears. A twitching nose. It couldn't be, could it?

'Hey!' he shouted joyfully. 'It's the rabbit! He escaped!'

He'd found a home with the wild bunnies. This place was a playground for rabbits – there was a maze of burrows under the dune grass.

The luminous rabbit had been very busy since he arrived. As Smiler and Coriander watched, some tiny baby bunnies came skipping out and surrounded him.

'*Awwww!*' said Smiler, with a soppy smile on his face. 'Can you believe that? He's a dad!'

Some of his children glowed. Some didn't. Before Coriander could tell him, Smiler got in first. 'It's the lottery of evolution,' he said.

Suddenly the proud, glowing dad started flashing on and off, like the light on top of a police car.

'I didn't know he could do that!' said Smiler, appalled. 'Why's he doing that?'

'Why do you think?' said Coriander. Lady rabbits were soon crowding round him, fluttering their eyelashes. They looked very impressed.

Smiler could guess what Coriander was going to talk about next. Superlice, modern humans, Neanderthals and now rabbits! He covered his ears.

'Just don't mention *mating* again!' Smiler warned her, squirming. 'I already know *all* there is to know about it. Right?'

Slime Alert!

Now that the superlice were dead, Smiler and Coriander thought they could relax. They were wrong. Other creatures had survived the wreck of the fort. They were the real enemy. They made Dr Maudlin's superlice seem about as dangerous as butterflies.

For a start, there were billions of them. Together, they seemed unstoppable. They could even survive underwater. Smiler and Coriander didn't know it, but an invading army was creeping towards the shore. It glowed ghostly green on the dark sea bed. It was the metal-eating Stone Age slime mould.

Millions of years ago, long before dinosaurs, slime moulds ruled the world. The earth was covered in slimy crusts, thick and wrinkled as elephant skin. Slime rule only ended when other creatures evolved, like shellfish and worms. They liked to eat slime mould for lunch.

The metal-eating slime mould wasn't in a rush. It kept stopping for a snack. There was loads of metal junk cluttering the sea bed. It polished off two supermarket trolleys and an old bicycle. They didn't hold it up for very long.

Like a shoal of microscopic piranhas, it surged over the wreck of a plane. It was a Messerschmidt the iron fort had shot down in World War II. When the mould had gobbled the plane, it flowed on. And, after every meal, it multiplied.

If it ever got to the mainland, there would be total chaos. Water pipes, electricity cables, cars, cutlery. These were just a few of the things it could munch up.

It would be the end of civilization as we know it. Could anything stop it?

Limpets could. Shellfish had helped bring the first Slimy Empire to an end. Now they were needed again.

While Smiler and Coriander cloud watched, a deadly battle was going on under the waves.

Who will win? Will limpets eat all the slime mould and save the world? Or will the slime reach the shore and set up Slimy Empire II?

Who knows what it'll munch first? It could be computer circuits. Or even railway lines. So look out for secret warning signs.

If computers start crashing or trains get delayed, you'll know the limpets lost.

Read more in Puffin

For complete information about books available from Puffin – and Penguin – and how to order them, contact us at the appropriate address below. Please note that for copyright reasons the selection of books varies from country to country.

www.puffin.co.uk

In the United Kingdom: Please write to Dept EP, Penguin Books Ltd, Bath Road, Harmondsworth, West Drayton, Middlesex UB7 ODA

In the United States: Please write to Penguin Putnam Inc., P.O. Box 12289, Dept B, Newark, New Jersey 07101–5289 or call 1–800–788–6262

In Canada: Please write to Penguin Books Canada Ltd, 10 Alcorn Avenue, Suite 300, Toronto, Ontario M4V 3B2

In Australia: Please write to Penguin Books Australia Ltd, P.O. Box 257, Ringwood, Victoria 3134

In New Zealand: Please write to Penguin Books (NZ) Ltd, Private Bag 102902, North Shore Mail Centre, Auckland 10

In India: Please write to Penguin Books India Pvt Ltd, 11 Panscheel Shopping Centre, Panscheel Park, New Delhi 110 017

In the Netherlands: Please write to Penguin Books Netherlands bv, Postbus 3507, NL–1001 AH Amsterdam

In Germany: Please write to Penguin Books Deutschland GmbH, Metzlerstrasse 26, 60594 Frankfurt am Main

In Spain: Please write to Penguin Books S. A., Bravo Murillo 19, 1° B, 28015 Madrid

In Italy: Please write to Penguin Italia s.r.l., Via Felice Casati 20, I–20124 Milano

In France: Please write to Penguin France S. A., 17 rue Lejeune, F–31000 Toulouse

In Japan: Please write to Penguin Books Japan, Ishikiribashi Building, 2–5–4, Suido, Bunkyo-ku, Tokyo 112

In South Africa: Please write to Longman Penguin Southern Africa (Pty) Ltd, Private Bag X08, Bertsham 2013